THE SNUGGLY
SATYRICON

EDITED, INTRODUCED AND TRANSLATED BY

BRIAN STABLEFORD

THIS IS A SNUGGLY BOOK

ISBN: 978-1-64525-021-0

THE SNUGGLY
SATYRICON

Brian Stableford's scholarly work includes *New Atlantis: A Narrative History of Scientific Romance* (Wildside Press, 2016), *The Plurality of Imaginary Worlds: The Evolution of French roman scientifique* (Black Coat Press, 2017) and *Tales of Enchantment and Disenchantment: A History of Faerie* (Black Coat Press, 2019). In support of the latter projects he has translated more than a hundred volumes of *roman scientifique* and more than twenty volumes of *contes de fées* into English. He has edited *Decadence and Symbolism: A Showcase Anthology* (Snuggly Books, 2018), and is busy translating more Symbolist and Decadent fiction.

His recent fiction, in the genre of metaphysical fantasy, includes a trilogy of novels set in West Wales, consisting of *Spirits of the Vasty Deep* (2018), *The Insubstantial Pageant* (2018) and *The Truths of Darkness* (2019), published by Snuggly Books, and a trilogy set in Paris and the south of France, consisting of *The Painter of Spirits*, *The Quiet Dead* and *Living with the Dead*, all published by Black Coat Press in 2019.

CONTENTS

INTRODUCTION

HOW many people, over the centuries, must have read the famous *Satyricon* attributed to Titus Petronius, more commonly known as Petronius Arbiter, and then thrown it away in disgust, having observed that although it is clearly advertised by its title as a book of satyrs, it does not feature any—not, at least, in a literal sense? That deceptive *Satyricon* is, in fact, a book of satire.

The confusion is understandable, as the word "satire" was often rendered "satyre" before the standardization of English spelling in the eighteenth century, and for a long time the French word *satyre* signified both satyr and satire. Modern etymologists assure us that the word "satire" does not, in fact, derive from the same root as "satyr," and as they claim to be experts, scholars, and even scientists, they naturally feel strongly that we ought to be obliged to take their word for it. On the other hand, there is some evidence that in the early days of Greek dramatic art, the performance of a tragedy was often followed by a "satyr play" in which actors travestied as satyrs replaced the solemn chorus of earnest explanation and lamentation in order to provide a measure of sarcastic comic relief, so it would not have been surprising if the idea of a "satyr play" had been transmuted over time into the more recent idea of a "satire." Scholars assure us that it did not happen, but scholars assure us of a lot of things that are mere guesswork on their part, relying on their prestige to carry conviction, in spite of the clear warnings issued by classical tragedy against the sin of hubris—which would probably have been mocked in satyr plays.

At any rate, the present volume is the first honest satyricon, featuring an entire chorus line of satyrs, fauns, aegipans and the Great God Pan himself—in whose divine image, of course, satyrs were made. Some of them, naturally, are made of stone or wood, sculpture being the principle means of transport by which the satyrs of antiquity have survived into the present day, but that does not prevent them from playing a role in human affairs. Does the volume also contain an element of satire? Of course it does, because—whatever etymology might allege—satyrs are inherently satirical. They are, in essence, travesties of human form, human appetite and human behavior—or, to be more specific, human male behavior; or, to be even more specific, male sexual behavior. Thus, satyrs also survive in metaphor, including medical metaphor, in such terms as satyriasis, and in the jesting wordplay of biological taxonomy, *Pan satyrus* being the quaintly insulting Linnaean classification of the chimpanzee.

The notion of a satyr is, inevitably, rather fluid; one of the great advantages of imaginary species—which allows them to thrive in the great struggle for memetic existence—is that they can easily be modified by further imagination. In classical terminology there is more than one species, although it profoundly unclear how fauns and aegipans differ from satyrs, and the companions of Dionysus, sometimes compressed by classical writers into the single individual Silenus, although that name probably applied originally to a species, are only distinguishable in being more gluttonous, fonder of alcohol and more loquacious. One of them is, however, memorably credited with most ancient item of wisdom to have been handed down to us from Arcadia, usually cited as "The best thing of all is not to be born, and after that to die young." Some literary modifiers, considering satyrs and fauns as if they were members of a biological species, have invented satyresses and faunesses, but traditionally, the objects of satyr lust were nymphs, especially dryads, by virtue of sharing a common habitat. Medical language, with typical bluntness and stupidity, echoes that assumption by calling the female equivalent of satyriasis nymphomania; both diseases are probably imaginary, but one could argue that the imaginary nature in question not inappropriate in itself.

Had satyrs been members of a biological species, it would have made little sense for them to lust after nymphs, human in form but not in nature, being more delicate as well as more ethereal, and there are not many mythological records of satyrs and nymphs producing offspring. The roots of myth are not to be sought in genetics, however, but in psychology; the fact that satyrs are perennially imagined as lying in wait for and attempting to force themselves upon reluctant nymphs reflects a common assumption about male and female attitudes to sex, satyrs being symbolic of frequent male behavior and nymphs of frequent female behavior.[1] Medical terminology is, in this regard, flagrantly ridiculous; "nymphomania" really ought to mean a horror of sex—but who expects sensibility from quacks?

Satyrs, therefore, are inherently symbolic, and they are symbolic with a nudge and a wink, because they are symbolic of male carnal lust, which is inherently absurd when it is not starkly tragic—and, in fact, also when it is. So, all of the stories in the present volume are about carnal pursuit, sometimes a trifle obliquely; all of them are tragic, and all of them also have an element of hilarity about their absurdity. As the popular saying has it: "You have to laugh, or you'd cry"—but like most popular sayings, that one has a hint of medical stupidity about it. So, reader, you can cry if you want to; in the immortal words of Seymour Gottlieb, as rendered by various nymphettes, it's your party.

Because satyrs are inherently symbolic, with the satirical nudge and wink built in, they had an inevitable appeal to the writers of the French *fin-de-siècle*, many of whom described themselves, a trifle redundantly, as "Symbolists," many of whom also liked to think of themselves as "Decadent" and many of whom also liked chasing "nymphs." They were almost all men—it is not surprising that the only story in the present volume that

---

1 I say "frequent" instead of "normal" because "normal" is a term coined by conformists is order to try to persuade persons given to mental independence that conformism is a virtue; it is a crucial element of the heavy artillery of linguistic tyranny, and has no place in any sort of Satyricon, except in the occasional sarcastic footnote.

might have been written by a woman is the one with an untraceable signature—and thus would have liked to be successful satyrs, but, being only writers, they were strong on theory but woefully weak in practice, thus failing to qualify for the diploma. Such is the tragedy of the pen, which, in spite of what writers would like to think, is definitely not mightier than the sword, especially metaphorically. If anyone ever doubts that there is many a true word spoken in jest, they need only consider the word "prick."

The Symbolist fantasies in the present volume, partly in consequence of that last remark, frequently have a component of wistfulness about their ambivalence. Sometimes the wistfulness is disguised, as it is in the masterpiece of the microsubgenre, Anatole's France's magisterial "Saint Satyr," in which the beatified satyr featured in the story—a continuation and amplification of a train of thought begun in the earlier "Amycus and Célestin"—becomes symbolic of the entire Golden Age of Arcadian magnificence, when Pan was notionally omnipotent. In the story, the tomb of Saint Satyr bears no further inscription, but in the most nakedly satirical of the stories included here, Jules Laforgue's account of the archetypal legend of the archetype of the satyrs, a mysterious tomb is introduced simply in order to enable the author to cite the most famous epitaph in French mortuary architecture: *Et in Arcadia Ego*. That teasingly ambiguous phrase might serve as the motto for the entire microsubgenre, not only referring literally to the mythological roots of the fantasies but also to an essential bitter nostalgia in their dominant tone.

Although the physical differences between them are imperceptible and the categories overlap considerably, fauns are usually conceived in milder, more sympathetic and more sentimental terms than satyrs. A key influence on the Symbolist imagery of the faun, if not the satyr, was Stéphane Mallarmé's poem "L'Apres-Midi d'un faune," known to the core members of the movement even before its initial publication in 1876 but extravagantly repopularized by the success of Claude Debussy's symphonic poem *Prélude à l'aprè-midi d'un faune*, premièred in Paris in 1894 and provided in 1912 with a legendary dance accompaniment by Vaclav Nijinsky. Prose developments of the motif in the present volume which follow that trend include those by Albert Samain and Maurice Magre, but some, like Remy de Gourmont's, deliberately oppose the ultra-Romanticization of the faun, exaggerating their affectation of prosaicism in apparent response. Most of the flesh-and-bone capripeds featured in the present volume are more crudely down-to-earth than Mallarmé's sentimental dreamer, although the stone specimens, perversely, sometimes borrow something of his ethereality.

That down-to-earth element notwithstanding, writers in general, and Symbolists in particular, have always sided with the imagination against the supposed brutality of realism, often resenting science for its alleged demystification of beautiful belief, as in John Keats' notorious indictment of Isaac Newton for "unweaving the rainbow." All of the stories collected here were written in a particular historical phase of that regretful reaction, when the idea of the satyr was frequently treated as an item of belief whose inevitable decay, however just and accurate, involved an element of loss. That is, of course, a myth in itself. There never was a time when anyone believed in satyrs, any more than anyone ever believed, let alone lived, in Arcadia. Satyrs were always products of the conscious imagination, aspects of the apparatus of deliberate storytelling, inherently symbolic and sarcastic, aspects of a vast choral society of voices in a virtual wilderness that exists in parallel with brutal reality, more colorful, more honest and more meaningfully musical, even—perhaps especially—when deliberately discordant.

The whole point of a chorus of satyrs, appended to the tragedy of actual life—viewed Silenically—is that they sang out of tune and danced clumsily, on cloven hooves instead of ballet shoes. They were not refined. Nymphs were ultra-refined, satyrs were ultra-unrefined, and that was the essence of their juxtaposition—a juxtaposition entailing an eternal pursuit that, even if it sometimes ended, usually concluded in rape and tragedy, not in fertility. Real life, Silenus would probably have pointed out, after an alcoholic burp, is frequently similar, in spite of all the efforts of morality to refine it, with the ardent collaboration of writers—even Symbolists—and the extraordinarily elaborate mythology of romantic love. That mythology has undergone a spectacular evolution since the days of Aphrodite and Eros, when it was an essentially insensate affliction employed by the gods— among many other weapons of nasty psychological warfare—to punish hubris. In spite of that evolution, one conspicuous absurdity, in antiquity and modernity alike, is that of a satyr in love—which is why most of the stories in this Satyricon treat the notion with hilarious irony, Albert Samain's hybrid Hyalis being an exception, at the opposite end of the spectrum from Léon Cladel's aegipan.

Modern Satyrs, therefore—and all the satyrs in the present Satyricon are quintessentially modern—are complex figures clad in several layers of myth, all of them in conflict with themselves as well as one another. In that context, wistfulness is absurd, but in that context, absurdity is far closer to truth and reality than the artificial "reality" constructed by that great oxymoron "common sense." The great virtue of satyrs, partly but not entirely because they allegedly have no truck with virtue, has always been that they are paradoxical. And the great virtue of modern literary satyrs, partly but not entirely because an anathema has been pronounced against them by fans of literary "realism," is that they are doubly or triply paradoxical, contradictions lurking within contradictions: ideal material for irony, satire and the curious nostalgic wistfulness that writers often feel when they regret a literary Golden Age that never was and never will be, when the censors and would-be castrators of the imagination—which do not in fact, include science—were or might be less insistent.

There are a few refrains that recur in the following chorus, as is necessarily the case in any singalong, but they are all played on different instruments, none of which is a simple reed pipe, and although they mostly attempt to harmonize with their immediate neighbors, they all try to avoid marching to the beat of the charivari of conventional thought. What effect the ensemble will have remains uncertain because, as previously noted, this is the first ever true Satyricon. Think of it, if you like, as an experiment, and yourself as an eager investigator—the Arbiter, if you will—anxious to discover the result and weigh the balance of laughter and tears, but hopefully ready, if the occasion warrants it, to cry "Io Pan!"

THE SNUGGLY
SATYRICON

SAINT SATYR

by Anatole France

Consors paterni luminis,
Lux ipse lucis et dies,
Noctem canendo rumpimus:
Assiste postulantibus.

Aufer tenibras mentium;
Fuga catervas daemonum;
Expelle somnolentiam,
Ne pigritantes obruat.[1]
(Breviarum Romanum.
Third Day of the Week: at Matins.)

FRA MINO had elevated himself above his brothers by means of his humility; although he was still young he governed the monastery of Santa Fiora wisely. He was pious. He took pleasure in prolonging his meditations

---

1 Consort of the Father's light, Light of light and day, We interrupt the evening with prayers: Help us, Thy suppliants. Remove darkness from our minds; Scatter the demon hosts; Expel somnolence, Lest we weaken in our duty to Thee.

and his prayers; sometimes he had ecstatic visions. After the fashion of St. Francis, his spiritual father, he composed songs in the language of the common people to celebrate that perfect love which is the love of God. Those works were without any fault of meter or meaning, for he had studied the seven liberal arts at the University of Bologna.

One evening, while Fra Mino was walking under the arches of the cloister, he felt his heart fill up with confusion and sadness at the memory of a Florentine lady whom he had loved when he was in the first flower of his youth, before the habit of St. Francis had extended its protection to his flesh. He begged God to expel that image, but sorrow remained in his heart.

The bells, he thought, *say as the angels do: Ave Maria; but their voice fades away in the mists of the heavens. On the wall of this cloister, the master honored by Perouse has painted a marvelous picture of the Marys contemplating the body of the Savior with an inexpressible love; but darkness has veiled the tears in their eyes and the mute sobs of their mouths, and I cannot weep with them. That well, in the middle of the courtyard, was covered just now with doves which had come to drink, but they have flown away, having found no water in the hollow of the curb-stone. Witness, Lord, that my soul is hushed like the bells, cloaked by darkness like the Marys, and dried up like the well. Why, Divine Jesus, is my heart arid, tenebrous and mute, when you are its dawning light, its birdsong and the spring descending from the hills?*

He dreaded returning to his cell and, thinking that prayer would dissipate his sorrow and calm his anxiety, he went through the low door of the cloister into the convent's church. Mute darkness filled the edifice, built more than five hundred years before on the remains of a Roman temple by the great Margaritone.[1] Fra Mino traversed the nave and went to kneel down in the chapel of the apse, dedicated to St. Michael, whose legend was painted on the wall, although the dim light of the lamp suspended from the vault did not permit him to see the archangel combating the demon and weighing souls. The moon, however, sent through the window a silvery beam that fell upon the tomb of Saint Satyr, placed in an arcade to the right of the altar. That tomb, shaped like a wine-vat, was far older than the church, and closely resembled a pagan sarcophagus, save for the fact that the sign of the Cross was inscribed in triplicate on its marble walls.

Fra Mino remained prostrate before the altar for some considerable time, but it proved impossible for him to pray, and in the middle of the night he felt that he was weighed down by the same torpor that had overwhelmed Christ's disciples in the Garden of Olives. And while he remained extended, devoid of courage and discretion, he saw something like a white cloud rising up above the tomb of Saint Satyr. He soon realized that the cloud in question was made up of a multitude of clouds, each of which was a woman. They floated in the dark air, and their lithe bodies shone through their flimsy tunics; and Fra Mino saw that there were young men among them

---

1 The thirteenth-century painter Margaritone d'Arezzo, best-known for a painting of St. Francis.

with the feet of goats, who were pursuing them. Their nudity allowed the frightful ardor of their desire to be manifest; however, the nymphs fled, and flowers and streams were born beneath their rapid feet. Every time a capriped extended his hand towards one of them and thought that he could seize her, a willow-tree suddenly shot up to hide the nymph within its hollow trunk as in a cavern, and its pale foliage filled with light murmurs and mocking laughter.

When all the women were hidden in the willows, the capripeds, sitting on the sodden grass, blew into their reed pipes and drew sounds therefrom by which any creature might have been troubled. The charmed nymphs put their heads out of the branches, and little by little, quitting their shady retreats, they drew closer, attracted by the irresistible fluting. Then the goat-men threw themselves upon them with a demonic fury. In the arms of the insolent aggressors, the nymphs strove momentarily to jeer and mock; then they were no longer laughing. With their heads thrown back and their eyes drowned with joy and horror, they called to their mother, or cried: "I'm dying," or maintained a grim silence.

Fra Mino wanted to turn his head away, but he could not do it, and his eyes remained open in spite of his efforts.

Meanwhile, the nymphs, having knotted their arms around the loins of the capripeds, bit, caressed and irritated their hairy lovers and, mingled with them, enveloped them, bathed them with their own undulating flesh, livelier than the water of the stream that ran nearby beneath the willows.

At that sight, Fra Mino fell into sin, in spirit and intention. He longed to be one of those demons, half men and half beasts, and to hug to his bosom, in their fashion the Florentine lady whom he had loved in the days of his youth, but who was dead.

But already the goat-men were dispersing into the country. Some were collecting honey from the trunks of oak-trees, others were carving reeds into the form of pipes, or, bounding towards one another, were clashing their horned heads together. The inert bodies of the nymphs, delightfully exhausted by amour, were strewn about the meadow. Fra Mino groaned on the stone floor, for the desire to sin had been so fervent within him that now he was feeling entirely ashamed.

Suddenly, one of the recumbent nymphs, having chanced to turn her gaze toward him, cried: "A man! A man!"

And, her finger pointing him out to her companions, she said:

"Look, my sisters, that's no goatherd! No reed pipe can be seen beside him. Nor do I recognize him as the master of one of the rustic domains whose little gardens, suspended on the hillside over the vines, are guarded by a Priapus carved from the trunk of a beech. What is he doing among us if he is neither a goatherd, nor an oxherd, nor a gardener? His expression is somber and severe, and I cannot read in his eyes the love of the gods and goddesses who populate the great heavens, the woods and the mountains. He is dressed in a barbaric fashion. Perhaps he is a Scythian. Let's approach this stranger, my sisters, and make certain that he has not come in enmity to foul our fountains, fell our trees, tear open our mountain-sides and reveal to cruel men the mystery of our fortunate refuges. Come with me, Mnaïs; come, Aglaia, Naera and Melibea."

"Let's go!" replied Mnaïs. "Let's go, fully armed!"

"Let's go!" they all cried, in unison.

And Fra Mino saw that, having got to their feet, they were gathering roses by the handful, and they advanced towards him in a long line, armed with roses and thorns. But the distance which separated him from them—which had seemed small at first, for he thought that he could almost touch them, and feel their breath upon his flesh, suddenly seemed to increase, and he saw them coming as if from a distant forest. Impatient to reach him, they broke into a run, menacing him with their thorny flowers. Threats also spilled from their flowery lips; but as they came closer, a change came over them; with every step they took they lost something of their grace and brilliance.

The gloss of their youth faded while the bouquets of roses withered in their hands. To begin with, their eyes became hollow and their mouths subsided. Their necks, so recently pure and white, became deeply creased; locks of gray hair trailed over their wrinkled foreheads. As they came further, their eyes became bloodshot, their lips drew back to their toothless gums. They came further still, carrying dried-out roses in their black arms, twisted like the old vines which the peasants of Chianti feed to their fires on winter nights. And still they came on, shaking their heads and trembling on their spindly legs.

When they reached the place where Fra Mino was pinned down by fright they were no more than horrible witches, bald and bearded, with great hooked noses and flabby, pendulous breasts. They crowded around him.

"Oh, the little darling!" said one. "He's as white as a sheet, and his heart is beating like that of a hare bitten by dogs. Aglaia, my sister, what should we do with him?"

"My dear Naera," Aglaia replied, "we ought to open his breast, take out his heart, and put a sponge in its place."

"Not at all," said Melibea. "That would make him pay too dearly for his curiosity and for the pleasure he had in surprising us. It's sufficient, this time, to inflict a lighter punishment. Let's give him a good spanking."

Immediately, surrounding the monk, the sisters pulled his robe over his head, and beat him with the sheaves of thorns which they still had in their hands.

Blood had begun to flow when Naera gave the signal to desist.

"Enough!" she said. "This is my admirer! I saw right away that he looked at me tenderly, and I want to satisfy his desires by giving myself to him without further delay."

She smiled: a single long black tooth, which projected from her mouth, tickled his nose. She murmured: "Come to me, my Adonis!" Then, suddenly furious, she cried: "Damn it! His senses are numb. His coldness is an affront to my beauty. He's scorning me; avenge me, my companions! Mnaïs, Aglaia, Melibea, avenge your sister!"

At that appeal, they all lifted their thorny scourges, and chastised the unfortunate Fra Mino so severely that his entire body was soon nothing but a wound. They stopped occasionally to cough and spit, but then recommenced plying their switches more ardently than before. They did not stop until they were exhausted.

"I hope," said Naera, then, "that next time he won't insult me in the unmerited fashion that still makes me blush. Let's leave him his life. But if he betrays the secret of our games and pleasures, we'll strike him dead. *Au revoir*, little darling!"

Having said that, the old woman crouched down over the monk and inundated him with a noxious liquid. Each of her sisters did the same, and then they returned, one after another, to the tomb of Saint Satyr, which they entered by means of a tiny crack in the lid, leaving their victim lying in a puddle which stank unbearably.

When the last one had disappeared, the cock crowed. Fra Mino was finally able to get up from the ground. Worn out by fatigue and pain, numb with cold, shivering with fever, half-suffocated by the exhalations of the poisonous liquid, he adjusted his clothing and dragged himself to his cell as dawn broke.

From that night on, Fra Mino could no longer find repose. The memory of what he had seen in Saint Michael's chapel, on Saint Satyr's tomb, troubled him during services and private prayers alike. He trembled when he accompanied the brethren into the church.

When he was required by the Rule to kiss the pavement of the choir, his terrified lips discovered traces of the nymphs there, and he murmured: "My Savior, do you not hear me saying to you what you once said to your Father: Lead us not into temptation?"

He had thought at first of sending the bishop an account of what he had seen, but on due reflection he convinced himself that it would be better to meditate upon these extraordinary events at his leisure, and not make them public until he had made a more exact study of them. It transpired, moreover, that the bishop, allied with the Guelphs of Pisa against the Ghibellines of Florence, was presently engaged in waging war so fervently that he had scarcely taken his armor off for a month. That is why, without speaking to anyone else, Fra Mino undertook profound research regarding the tomb of Saint Satyr and the chapel in which it was contained. Well-versed in the study of books, he leafed through the ancient and the modern, but did not find any enlightenment. The treatises on Magic that he studied only served to redouble his uncertainty.

One morning, when he had, as usual, worked all night, he tried to raise his spirits by taking a walk in the country. He took an uphill path that, winding between vines clinging to elm-trees, led to a wood of myrtles and olives, once held sacred by the Romans. His feet in the damp grass, his brow refreshed by the dew dripping from the wayfaring trees, Fra Mino had been walking in the forest for a long time when he came upon a spring over which tamarisks gently dangled their light foliage and feathery clusters of pink berries. Lower down, in a pool among the willows, motionless herons could be seen. Little birds were singing among the branches of the myrtles. The moist scent of mint rose up from the ground, and the grass was spangled with the flowers of which Our Lord said: "Solomon in all his glory was not clad like one of these."[1] Fra Mino sat down on a mossy stone and, praising the God who had made the sky and the dew, he meditated upon the hidden mysteries of Nature.

Because the memory of what he had seen in the chapel never left him, he lowered his head into his hands, asking himself for the thousandth time what the dream signified. *For such a vision*, he said to himself, *must have a meaning; it might even have several, which it is important to discover, if not by sudden illumination then by the precise application of the rules of scholarship. And I assume that in this particular case the poets I have studied at Bologna, the likes of the satirist Horace and Statius, ought to be of considerable help to me, given that so much truth is buried in their fables.*

Having considered those notions for some time, and others more subtle still, he looked up, and found that he was not alone. Leaning against the cavernous trunk of an ancient ilex, an old man was gazing up through the foliage at the sky, and smiling. Blunt horns projected from his hoary brow. A white beard hung down from his flat-snouted face, through which the folds of his neck could be seen. Shaggy hair covered his chest. From his thighs to his cloven feet he was covered by a thick

---

1 *Matthew* 6:29, referring to "the lilies of the field."

fleece. He held a reed pipe up to his lips, from which he extracted a faint tune. Then he sang, in a voice hardly distinguishable from the music:

She fled, laughing,
Chewing the golden grapes.
But I caught up with her easily,
And my teeth crushed
The cluster on her mouth.

Having seen and heard those things, Fra Mino made the sign of the cross. But the old man was not at all troubled by it, and he fixed the monk with an ingenuous stare. Amid the deep lines of his face, his clear blue eyes sparkled like the water of a spring between the bark of oak trees.

"Whether you are man or beast," cried Mino, "I command you in the name of the Savior to tell me who you are."

"My son," replied the old man, "I am Saint Satyr! Lower your voice, lest you frighten the birds."

Fra Mino went on, in a more moderate tone: "Old man, since you have not fled the redoubtable sign of the cross, I can no longer think that you are a demon or some impure spirit escaped from Hell. But if, as you say, you are truly a man, or rather the soul of a man sanctified by a life of good works and by the favor of Our Lord, I wish that you would explain to me the marvel of your goat's horns and those shaggy legs, which terminate in black cloven hooves."

In response to this question the old man lifted his arms towards the heavens, and said: "My son, the nature of men, animals, plants and stones is the secret of the immortal gods, and I know no more than you do about the origin of these horns which deck my forehead, upon which the nymphs once used to hang garlands of flowers. I don't know what these folds of flesh are that droop from my neck, or why I have the feet of an audacious goat. I can only tell you, my son, that there were once women in these woods who had horned brows and hairy shanks like mine, although their breasts were round and white and their bellies and their hairy loins gleamed. The sun was young then, and loved to dapple them with its golden rays as they sheltered beneath the foliage. They were beautiful, my son! Alas, they have vanished from the woods, every last one. The others of my kind perished with them, and today I am the only one of my kind. I'm very old."

"Old man, tell me the age that gave birth to you, your ancestry and your fatherland."

"My son, I was born of the Earth long before Saturn was dethroned by Jupiter, and my eyes have contemplated the flourishing novelty of the world. The human race had not yet emerged from the clay. Alone with me, the dancing satyresses made the ground reverberate with the rhythm of their twin hooves. They were taller, more robust and more beautiful than nymphs or women, and their ample loins received in abundance the seed of the first-born of the Earth.

"Under the reign of Jupiter, the nymphs began to inhabit the springs, the woods and the mountains. Fauns, mingling with the nymphs, formed light choirs deep in the woods. Meanwhile, I lived happily, consuming at my leisure the wild grapes and the lips of the laughing faunesses. I savored peaceful sleep in the thick grass. I celebrated on my reed pipe Jupiter after Saturn, because it is within me to praise the gods, masters of the world.

"Alas, I have grown old, for I am only a god, and the centuries have bleached the hairs upon my head and upon my breast; they have extinguished the ardor of my loins. I was already weighed down by age when great Pan died and when Jupiter, suffering the fate that he had inflicted on Saturn, was dethroned by the Galilean. I dragged from then on a life so languid, that I eventually died and was placed in my tomb. Truly, I am now but a shadow of my former self. If I still exist a little, it is because nothing is ever really lost, and it is not permitted to anyone to die completely. Death cannot be more perfect than life. My child, the beings which are lost in the ocean of things are like the waves that you can see rising and falling in the Adriatic Sea. They have neither a beginning nor an end, they are born and they die insensibly, as insensibly as my soul drains away. A faint memory of the satyresses of the Golden Age still animates my eyes, and from my lips the ancient hymns still silently take flight."

Having said all that, he fell silent.

Fra Mino looked at the old man, and knew that he was nothing but a phantom.

"It is not entirely incredible," he said, "that you are a capriped without being a demon. The creatures that God formed in order to have no part in Adam's heritage can no more be damned than they can be saved. I do not believe that the centaur Chiron, who was wiser than any man, suffers eternal punishment in the jaws of Leviathan. A traveler who penetrated into Limbo says that he had seen him seated on the grass, conversing with Ripheus, the most righteous of the Trojans. Although others declare that Paradise itself has been opened to Ripheus of Troy,[1] it is permissible to entertain doubts regarding the matter. Nevertheless, old man, you lied when you told me that you were a saint, you who are not even a man."

The capriped replied: "My son, when I was young, I did not lie any more than the ewes whose milk I sucked or the goats with which I butted heads, glorying in my strength and my beauty. In those days, nothing lied, and the fleeces of sheep had not yet found out how to be remade in deceptive colors; I have not changed my nature in the intervening years; you can see that I am as naked as I was in Saturn's Golden Age. My spirit is no more veiled than my body. I do not lie. And why should you find it extraordinary, my son, that I have become a saint before the Galilean, without having emerged from the mother whom some call Eve and others Pyrrha, and who merits veneration under either name? Saint Michael was not born of woman either. I know him, and we have sometimes conversed together. He tells me about the time when he was an oxherd on Mount Gargan."

Fra Mino interrupted the satyr, saying: "I cannot allow Saint Michael to be described as an oxherd simply

1 Dante admits the Trojan hero Ripheus to Paradise in the *Comoedia*.

because he once kept watch over the cattle of a man named Gargan, like the mountain. But tell me, old man, how you came to be canonized."

"Listen," the capriped replied, "and your curiosity will be satisfied. When men came from the East to the placid Arno valley, bringing the news that the Galilean had dethroned Jupiter, they felled the oaks where the peasants suspended little clay goddesses and votive tablets; they planted crosses over the sacred springs and forbade the shepherds to carry their offerings of wine, milk and cakes to the grottos of the nymphs. The population of fauns, pans and sylvans rightly took offense. In their anger, they attacked the advocates of the new god. At night, when the apostles were asleep on their beds of dry leaves, nymphs came to pull their beards, and young fauns slipped into their stables to pull hairs out of their asses' tails. I tried in vain to disarm their ingenuous malice, and exhorted them to accept the new order. 'My children,' I said to them, 'the era of facile games and mocking laughter is past.' But they were imprudent, and would not listen. They brought misfortune on themselves.

"For myself, having seen the end of Saturn's reign I found it natural and just that Jupiter should perish in his turn. I was resigned to the fall of the great gods. I did not resist the emissaries of the Galilean. I even served them in small ways. Knowing the woodland paths better than they did, I gathered mulberries and little plums, which I left on beds of leaves on the threshold of their grotto. I also left offerings of plovers' eggs. And when they were building a cabin I carried wood and stones for them upon my back. In return, they anointed my forehead with water, and wished me the peace of Jesus Christ. I lived with them and like them. Those who loved them, loved me. Just as they were honored, I was honored in my turn, and my sanctity appeared to be equal to theirs.

"I have told you, my son, that I was already very old then. The sun hardly warmed my numb limbs. I was no better than an old hollow tree that could no longer put forth a crown of fresh leaves, deserted by the songbirds. Every return of autumn increased my decrepitude. One winter morning I was found stretched out, motionless, beside the road.

"The bishop, followed by his priests and all the people, held a funeral mass for me. Then I was placed in a huge tomb of white marble, marked three times with the sign of the cross, which bore on the front wall the name of SAINT SATYR in a garland of grapes.

"In those days, my son, tombs were built by the roadside. Mine was situated two miles from the city, on the road to Florence. A young plane-tree grew up over it, and covered it with a shadow dappled with sunlight, full of murmurous birdsong, freshness and joy. Not far away, a spring flowed over a bed of water-cress; boys and girls came to bathe together, laughing all the while. It was a charming place, and a holy one. Young mothers brought their babies there and made them touch the marble of the monument, in order that all their limbs might grow strong and straight. It was commonly believed that the newly-born brought to my sepulcher would one day surpass their fellows in vigor and courage. For that reason, the flower of the noble Tuscan race was brought to me. The peasants also brought me their she-donkeys, in the hope of making them fecund. My memory was revered. Every year, at the beginning of spring, the bishop would come with his clergy to pray over my remains, and I watched from afar the procession of crosses and candles through the meadows, with scarlet canopies, singing psalms. That was the way it was, my son, in the times of good King Berengar.[1]

"Meanwhile, the satyrs and satyresses, the fauns and the nymphs, dragged out a wandering and wretched life. For them, there were no more altars of meadow-grass, no more garlands of flowers, and no more offerings of milk, wheat and honey. Occasionally, some furtive goatherd would lay a little cheese on the threshold of a sacred grotto, whose entrance was being enveloped by brambles and thorns, but the rabbits and the squirrels came to eat those poor offerings. The nymphs, inhabitants of forests and other gloomy places, had been driven from their haunts by the apostles who came from the East; and to make sure that they could not return to them the priests of the Galilean God poured holy water on the trees and the stones, pronounced magical incantations of a kind in which they were well-versed, and set up crosses where the forest paths met.

"The Galilean, my son, is well-versed in the art of incantations. He knows the virtue of formulae and signs better than Saturn and Jupiter. So the poor rustic divini-

---

1 Berengar I (c845-924) became the ruler of Italy in 883 and Holy Roman Emperor in 915.

ties could no longer take shelter in their sacred groves; the chorus of shaggy capripeds, who once had stirred the maternal earth with their rhythmic feet, was no more than a host of pale, mute shadows, trailing the hillsides like the morning mist that is dissipated by the sun.

"Buffeted by the wrath of Heaven, as if by a furious wind, those specters swirled all day long in the dust of the highways. Night was a little less hostile to them, for night did not entirely belong to the Galilean god; the demons had their share of its dominion. When the shadow of night descended from the hills, fauns and faunesses, nymphs and pans, came to cower beside the tombs which bordered the roads, and there, under the mild empire of the infernal powers, they would enjoy a brief repose. They preferred my tomb to the others, because it was that of a venerable ancestor. Soon they all gathered together under the part of the cornice which was always dry and free of moss because it faced south. The folk of the air flew to it faithfully every night, like doves to a dovecote. They found space there easily enough, having become very tiny, as light as the chaff blown away by the winnowing-fan. For myself, emerging from my mute chamber, I came to sit down in their midst, under cover of the marble tiles, and I sang to them, in a faint, whispering voice, about the days of Saturn and Jupiter; and it reminded them of the lost felicity. With Diana looking down on them they would devote themselves to the image of their ancient frolics, and belated travelers would think that they had seen the mists of the moonlit meadows imitating the mingled bodies of lovers. In fact, they were little more than light mist themselves. The cold made them very ill.

"One night, when the snow had covered the countryside, the nymphs Aglaia, Naera, Mnaïs and Melibea slipped through cracks in the marble into the narrow and gloomy chamber I inhabit. Their companions came crowding after them, and the fauns, bounding in pursuit of them, soon came to join them. My abode became theirs. We rarely left it, save to go into the woods on fine nights. Even then they would make haste to return before cock-crow; for you must understand, my son, that of all the horned race, I alone have leave to appear on earth during the daylight hours. It is a privilege granted to me by virtue of my sainthood.

"My sepulcher inspired more reverence than ever among the country folk, and every day the young mothers presented their nurslings to me, lifting up their naked bodies. When the Franciscan brothers established themselves in the country and built a monastery on the hillside they asked the archbishop if he would permit them to remove my tomb to the church and keep it there. This favor having been granted to them, I was transferred with much ceremony to the chapel of Saint Michael, where I still repose. My rustic family was brought here with me. It was a great honor, but I must admit that I missed the broad highway where, every daybreak, I could watch the peasant women carrying baskets of grapes, figs and aubergines on their heads. Time has hardly soothed my regrets at all, and I wish that I were still beneath the plane-tree on the sacred path.

"Such is my life," concluded the old capriped. "It flows on happily, gently and unobtrusively through all the ages of the earth. If a little sadness is mingled with its joy, that must be the will of the gods. Oh, my son, let us praise the gods, the masters of the world!"

Fra Mino was pensive for a while, and then said: "I now understand the meaning of what I saw, during a bad night, in the chapel of Saint Michael. But there is still one point about which I am unclear. Tell me, Old One, why the nymphs who dwell with you and who give themselves to the fauns were changed into disgusting old women when they came towards me."

"Alas, my son," replied Saint Satyr, "time spares neither men nor gods. The latter are immortal only in the imagination of ephemeral mankind. In reality, they feel the effects of age, and tend to decline irreparably as the centuries go by. Nymphs grow old as women do; as every rose withers to a husk, so every nymph withers into a witch. When you watched the frolics of my little family you could see how, even now, the memory of their youth still embellishes nymphs and satyrs when they make love, and how their briefly reanimated ardor can renew their charms—but the ruination of the centuries reappears immediately afterwards, alas. Unfortunately, the race of nymphs is ancient and decrepit."

Fra Mino asked again: "Old man, if it is true that you have achieved beatitude by mysterious ways, and if it is true, although absurd, that you are a saint, why do you remain in the tomb with these phantoms who do not know how to praise God, and whose indecency pollutes the house of the Lord. Respond, old man!"

But the capriped saint, without responding, vanished quietly into the air.

Seated on the mossy stone beside the spring, Fra Mino meditated upon the discourse which he had just heard, and found in it—albeit mingled with certain deep obscurities—a marvelous enlightenment.

This Saint Satyr, he thought, *is comparable to the Sibyl who, in a temple of the false gods, announced the coming of the savior to the nations. The mud of ancient lies still clings to his cloven hooves, but his forehead is raised towards the light, and his lips confess the truth.*

As the shadow of the beeches extended across the grass of the hillside the monk got up from his stone and went down the narrow path which led to the convent of the Franciscan brothers. But he dared not look at the water-lilies asleep upon the ponds, because they reminded him of the nymphs. He re-entered his cell at the very moment when the bells began to sound the Ave Maria. The cell was small, with whitened walls; its only furniture was a bed, a stool and a tall writing-desk. On the wall, a mendicant friar had once painted, in the manner of Giotto, the Marys at the foot of the Cross. Below that painting a wooden shelf, as black and lustrous as the beams of a wine-press, bore books, some of which were sacred and the others profane, for Fra Mino studied the ancient poets, in order to praise God in all the works of men, blessing Virgil the Mantuan for having prophesied the birth of the Savior in declaring to the nations of the world: *Jam redit et Virgo.*[1]

On the window-sill a long-stemmed lily protruded from a vase of unglazed earthenware. Fra Mino loved to trace the name of the holy Virgin inscribed in the

---

1 The Virgin also returns.

golden dust of the flower's corolla. The window, set high in the wall, was not large, but through it one could see the sky above the violet hills.

Having enclosed himself in the peaceful tomb to which he had committed his life and his desires, Mino stationed himself at the narrow desk with the two surmounting shelves, where he was accustomed to devote himself to his studies. There, dipping his reed-pen into the inkwell fastened to the side of the bank of pigeonholes which held his sheets of parchment, brushes, pigments and powdered gold, he prayed, in the name of the Lord, that the flies would not pester him, and he began to write an account of all that he had seen and heard in the chapel of Saint Michael during that misfortunate night, and what had transpired on that very day beside the spring in the wood. To begin with, he wrote these lines upon the parchment:

This is what Fra Mino, of the order of Minor Friars, has seen and heard, which he is relating for the instruction of the faithful. In praise of Jesus Christ and the glory of His blessed and humble follower, St. Francis. Amen.

Then he set down in writing, omitting nothing, what he had observed of the nymphs who became witches, and the old man with horns whose voice murmured in the woods as if it were the last sigh of the flute of antiquity, and a prelude to the sacred harp. While he wrote, the birds sang. Night came slowly to efface the lovely colors of the day. The monk lit his lamp and continued to write. As he reported the marvels with which he had become acquainted, he explained their literal and spiritual meanings, in accordance with the rules of scholarship. And, as if he were building a wall to fortify a town, he supported his arguments with texts taken from the Scriptures. From the singular revelations which he had received he deduced these conclusions:

Firstly, that Jesus Christ is Lord of all creatures, and is the God of satyrs and fauns as well as men; that is why Saint Jerome saw in the desert centaurs who confessed their faith in Jesus Christ.

Secondly, that God communicated to the pagans certain glimmerings of truth, in order that they might be saved; thus the sibyls, such as the Cumaean, the Egyptian and the Delphic, caused to appear, in the darkness of the gentiles, the Crib, the Rods, the Reed Scepter, the Crown of Thorns and the Cross—for which reason Saint Augustine had admitted the Erythrean sibyl into the City of God.

Fra Mino gave thanks to God for having been shown these things. A great joy flooded his heart at the thought that Virgil was among the elect. And he wrote with gladness at the bottom of the last page:

Here ends the Apocalypse of Friar Mino, humble follower of Jesus Christ. I have seen the holy aureole upon the horned head of the Satyr, signifying that Jesus Christ has brought forth from Limbo the sages and poets of antiquity.

The night was already well advanced when, having completed his task, Fra Mino stretched himself out on his bed to take a little rest. Just as he was dropping off to sleep an old woman came in through the window, borne by a moonbeam. He recognized her as the most horrible of the witches whom he had seen in the chapel of Saint Michael.

"My darling," she said to him, "what have you been doing today? We warned you, my gentle sisters and I, not to reveal our secrets, for if you betrayed us, we would kill you. And I would be afflicted by that, for I love you tenderly."

She took him in her arms, called him her celestial Adonis and her little white donkey, and covered him with ardent kisses.

When he pushed her away in disgust, she said to him: "Child, you treat me with disdain because my eyes are bloodshot, my nostrils corroded by the acrid and putrid fluid which they distill, and my gums garnished by a single tooth, which is black and unnaturally long. It is true that this is the state into which your Naera has fallen. But if you love me, I will become again, through you and for you, that which I was in the Golden Age of Saturn, when I was in the full flower of my youth, and the world itself was young and flourishing. It is amour, my young god, that makes the beauty of things. It only requires a little courage to make me beautiful. Get up, Mino, and display your virility!"

At these words, accompanied by gestures, Fra Mino, oppressed by terror and horror and dread, felt faint and slid from his bed on to the stone floor of his cell. As he fell, he thought he saw, between his half-closed eyelids, a perfectly-formed nymph, whose naked body flowed over him like spilled milk.

He woke in broad daylight, bruised from top to toe by his fall. The sheets of parchment which he had covered in ink during the night were scattered over the desk. He read them through, folded them up, secured them with sealing-wax and tucked them inside his robe. Heedless of the threats that the witches had made twice over, he went forth to carry his revelations to the bishop, the battlements of whose palace loomed up in the town center.

He found the bishop in the Great Hall, surrounded by men-at-arms, putting on his spurs; the pope had declared war upon the Ghibellines of Florence; he asked the monk to tell him the reason for his visit, and when he had been informed of it, he invited him to read out his account on the spot. Fra Mino obeyed. The bishop listened to the discourse until the end. He had no particular enlightenment on the subject of apparitions, but he was animated by an ardent zeal to protect the interests of the Faith. Without delaying for a single day, and without allowing the war to distract him from his purpose, he summoned twelve illustrious theologians and experts in canon law to hold an inquiry into the matter, and urged them to bring in their verdict.

After mature consideration, and not without subjecting Fra Mino to many interrogations, the scholars decided that it would be advisable to open the tomb of Saint Satyr in the chapel of Saint Michael, and subject it to a series of rites of exorcism. On the points of doctrine raised by Fra Mino they declined to issue a formal statement, although they were inclined to take the view that the Franciscan's arguments were temeritous, frivolous and unprecedented.

In conformity with the advice of the theologians, and by order of the bishop, the tomb of Saint Satyr was opened. It contained nothing but a few ashes, over which the priests sprinkled holy water. There arose in consequence a white vapor, from which feeble groans escaped.

On the night that followed the pious ceremony in question, Fra Mino dreamed that the witches, hovering over his bed, were tearing the heart out of him. He got up early in the morning, tormented by sharp pains and a raging thirst. He dragged himself as far as the well in the cloister, where the doves came to drink, but no sooner had he sipped the few drops of water which filled a hollow in the well-head than he felt his heart swell up like a sponge, and, murmuring "My God!" he choked to death.

AEGIPAN

by Léon Cladel

IN April, already nearly a quarter of a century ago, a landscape artist then ornamented by one of those heads of hair of which the Jeunes-France celebrated by Théophile Gautier, their master, were so proud, and no less bald today than the worst of those Philistines they abhorred *ex imo*, was surprised by nightfall in the mountains of Rouergue. There, all day long sitting under a willow umbelled like a parasol, he had attempted to sketch a truly classical location, which reminded him of some of the twenty-two canvases composing the *Life of Saint Bruno* painted by Eustache Lesueur, who, according to his biographers merited the title of the French Raphael.

Imagine a grim and deserted gorge between two long chains of rocks as perforated as madrepores, from which many springs escape in plaintive little cascades, which, joining up in the depths of a narrow valley, form a very impetuous torrent there, on the banks of which all kinds of vivacious herbs grow pell-mell. On one of the two walls, almost vertical, separated by the ravine, a ruined manor was profiled among the aromatic plants—species of thyme, mint and fennel—and on the other, the oblique fires of the setting sun enlivened the dead mosses covering the thatch of a sort of legendary hermitage, the last guest of which, quasi-centenarian, sieur Fra Coulas, deceased under the Restoration in an odor of sanctity, had never had a successor . . .

"Here, in truth, it's comfortable; since I'm here, I'll stay."

And the disciple of the likes of Millet, Corot, Troyon, Dupré and Courbet, after having shut his box of paints, his palette and his brushes, not feeling the strength to return to the inn in which he had been lodging for a few weeks, on the edge of a forest hamlet five or six kilometers away, had made his decision rapidly.

"The fresh and tender grass will serve as my bed, and the branches as my roof; there's a wedge of brown bread in my knapsack, with half a sausage, half a bottle of wine, dry cheese, and a flask of cheap brandy. Good God! Truly, that's more than I need to await the dawn as a sybarite, and even the imminent vespers."

Having installed himself tranquilly between two hedges, he attacked his provisions, and as soon as he was reinvigorated, stuffed his box-root pipe and smoked caporal, his eyes full of the wild rural splendors of the ambient nature, which gradually faded away . . .

"What chic, what elegance, all that has, damn it!"

Having seen the glorious sun set in floods of crimson and gold, and then the blessed moon rise, the diffuse light of which silvered the crests of the mountains and the abysms of the vales, he was getting ready to snore under the caress of the breezes and gaze at the stars when he heard the threading chromatic scales of a pipe to his right.

"To go to sleep to music, a real stroke of luck, yes—but where is it coming from?"

Raising himself up on his elbows and extending his head, he perceived a flock of goats conduced by a barbet descending the slope and getting ready to cross the stream on a tree-trunk; in the distance, through the ferns, precipitate footsteps sounded . . .

"After the flock, the dog and then the pastor; it's the order established since the commencement . . ."

He did not finish, and sat up, very astonished; in the half-light, he had distinguished at the foot of the slope a singular shadow, which was bounding with a vertiginous rapidity over the basalt blocs fallen from the ridge of the butte, and that phantom caught up with another, lighter, stopped in its course by an unexpected obstacle; then there was a rustle of cloth followed by shrill cries, and the starlight struck a flutter of dispersed veils . . .

"Was that a satyr? And his prey, a nymph? Are there still fauns and dryads in this country, then, and does old Pan still exist?"

Believing that he was the victim of his imagination, evoking involuntarily the beings that had populated antique regions resembling to some extent the landscape by which he was surrounded, the artist rubbed his eyes; a heart-rending plaint proved to him that he was not dreaming, and now he recognized a white nymph between the hairy arms of the goat-foot, who, having carried her toward a long fissure gaping at the base of one of the two mountains, plunged into it violently and disappeared with his victim, the black ravisher!

"Oh, that's too much, and I'm seeing things!"

Disturbed by that vision, although brave and not at all superstitious, having never been haunted by the mythological memories that he had once mocked with his studio comrades, the painter trembled all night, but as soon as day dawned, all his courage having returned to him, he explored the surroundings. No indication of abduction, no trace of nocturnal specters—except that, at the extremity of the fissure, he discovered in the middle of a thicket a shepherdess's crook broken into several pieces, and, further away, a clasp to which shreds of unbleached cloth were adhering, similar to that in which the surrounding peasants dressed in the warm season. Finally, on the threshold of the grotto, he stumbled over a walnut-wood clog too small for a man's foot, or even that of a mature woman. He wanted to enter the crypt that opened before him but could not.

He spotted some donkey drovers who were passing with their animals, rude Catalan mules laden with sacks of flour, while he was wondering, at the mouth of the cavern, whether there were troglodytes in that region, once inhabited by Ruthenians.

"Hey there, does anyone live here, by chance?"

Instead of responding they made the sign of the cross several times, and it was only from a distance that one of them, alarmed, shouted: "God protect you! Get away from there, that's the Spirits' hole!"

He drew away, very preoccupied. When he returned to the village he first questioned various artisans scarcely less illiterate than the local peasants, who nevertheless fell from the clouds after being amazed by his adventure, and then a few rather erudite bourgeois, including the local pharmacist, a member of several scientific societies, the author of pamphlets appreciated by the antiquarians and historians of the province, an ex-vice-president of committees of apiculture and taxidermy, etc. The admirers of the apothecary, and that phoenix himself, taking him for a madman, advised him ironically to consult the Eagle of the South-West, a certain bibliophile of Rodez who had at his fingertips all the facts and events of the Guyenne, Gascony and the entire Midi since the creation of our era, inclusively.

Very discontented with his investigation, and not very flattered to be the butt of the false commiseration of those villagers, as stupid as they were sly, the Parisian no longer breathed a word about his supposed fancies, and while cursing all of them internally, he continued as before to paint on mountains and in valleys the innumerable beauties of their harsh and magical land. Yes, but whether he was upstream or downstream of the torrential and sinuous Aveyron, on the edge of gulfs or on the aeries, here, there, everywhere and always, he was nonetheless harassed by the memory of the strange apparition in the course of the night spent in the open air, sometimes admitting that his senses had induced an error, and sometimes concluding, on the contrary, that they had not abused him.

Hazard finally took pity on his tiresome uncertainties and rid him of them. With his knapsack on his back and his staff in his hand, he was going down the peak of Jeül one evening when, the path winding around the flanks of that gigantic mound of quartz gneiss, a column of dust suddenly rose up and soon, shaking pitchforks and scythes, a caravan of peasants filed before him.

"We've got the werewolf," one of them growled. "And there he is!"

The pedestrian abused in that manner was walking in chains, with a rope around his neck, between two mounted gendarmes, pistols in their hands and swords drawn. Nothing was more extraordinary than that man of sorts, and one hesitated to believe that he was one. Clad in a sheepskin, the blue-tinted wool of which clung to his body, mingling with the hair of his bony chest, shod in woven horsehair under which his woolen flesh was irritated, he wore over his shoulder, at the end of a strap and over his cloak an assemblage of little wooden pipes of unequal length, equipped with metallic reeds.

His structure, even more unusual and savage than his accoutrement, was terrifying. In the middle of a long pale and curvilinear face bristling with stiff yellow hairs divided into two slack tufts, above a very brief chin, a huge hooked nose extended, quivering, scarcely interrupted by thick bulbous lips covering convex teeth embedded in bleeding gums; then, under a scarlet Béarnais beret, enveloping a receding brow, and two glittering glaucous eyes devoid of eyelashes or eyebrows, two protuberances extended, sharply pointed, like horns, one on either side projecting over soft narrow ears. The abnormal biped had rudimentary arms, very short, and his nostrils secreted a viscous fluid like that which spring from the muzzles of ruminants. That unusual being, which had no appreciable age, perched on two twisted legs, swollen at the hams, depressed at the knees and terminating in cloven feet with no appearance of toenails, advanced with the gait of a quadruped standing on its hind legs, and the boldness of the most salacious of beasts, the goat!

"Where the devil have I seen that muzzle before?" murmured the pupil of one of the foremost masters of the epoch in the art that he was learning. "Where, then, where?"

At that moment the sylvan turned his vitreous gaze toward a blonde girl squatting on a crumbling sandstone mound on the edge of the road and launched forward. Had it not been for the bonds attaching him to the pommels of the saddles, which retained him, he would have fallen upon her. Impotent and almost strangled, and pricked by the horsemen's spurs, he roared, frightening the horses, and bleated loudly.

"It's him! him!" cried the landscapist then, in a paroxysm of joy. "Oh, I suspected that I hadn't had a hallucination, in the dusk, in the forest, a few weeks ago. A visionary, me, never! Oh, *sacrebleu*, it's really him, my aegipan!"

And while someone recounted, at length, how that rugged and hairy monster, the issue of who knew what anthropomorphous beings, had been caught by night in a subterranean quarry, in the process of forcing two little girls as beautiful as the day, he quickly sharpened his pencils and not far away, in a village where they called a halt, he swiftly sketched that last son of the god of the woods, and it was those rapid notes that, later, were to furnish him with the principal lines of his unforgettable painting known to the artistic and literary public under the name by which this true story is titled, which I wrote under the eyes of the painter, facing his magnificent canvas, to which he will perhaps owe an immortality more durable than that of the late Monsieur X*** and so many other academicians, so completely dead today that no one in France, even in Paris, knows whether they lived.

THE FAUN

by Remy de Gourmont

SHE had retired early after dinner, believing that she was suffering, although she was only sad, weary of the excessively innocent laughter of the little children and the sanctimonious joviality of poor relatives excited by a little celebration.

Above all she was afflicted, almost indignantly, by the hypocritical tenderness that shone in her husband's dull eyes when there were people present; she would have preferred, like other wives, to be beaten in public and loved in secret.

Thanking her chambermaid, she drew the bolt, and then felt truly alone and less unhappy.

Undressing slowly, striking poses while glancing at the looking-glass, with feigned languor, as if falling adroitly into cherished arms, murmuring endearments to herself, offering a subtle compliment to her shoulder and even to her knee, and confessing that one has a beautiful soul and beautiful skin—she amused herself with all that, without thinking about anything wicked, with the security of a woman who has no fear of the surprises of the imagination.

Her ingenuous immodesty was limited by delicacy. She knew the level at which the tucked-up dress ought to stop, the water-level of dry weather and that of rainy days, and voluntarily, like Arlette when Robert the Devil favored her with his intimacy, she would have torn her chemise instead of taking it off. Nevertheless, she felt a slight shame, and, buried in a fur, she knelt down very chastely in front of the fire.

She poked the fire, rearranging the incandescent architecture; she burned her face, and became bored.

Would it not be better to respond to the hypocritical tenderness of her husband? With a few provocations she would have mastered herself and the evening would have finished in more calming exercises—whereas, troubled, enervated and irritated, she was capable of becoming melancholy to the point of tears and solitary sobs that nothing appeases, which wring the heart and agitate it like a piece of wreckage on a rough sea!

Oh, truly, the sad and stupid eve of Christmas! Were there, then, magical dates when it is a crime to be alone, when human contacts are necessary, under pain of suffering and almost of remorse? Such an idea was sketched momentarily in her feeble and mobile mind, but soon, of all that overly complicated design, only a single word remained visible to her eyes and sensible to her imagination: Christmas.

She became again a little girl going to midnight mass—in her bed, going to sleep dreaming of the pampering of the infant Jesus . . .

No, that's banal! Everyone has those visions of the past, such annual nostalgias! Undistinguished souls who are unable to evoke other dreams than those which roam everywhere, at the mercy of the most vulgar desires—docile and lamentable dreams!

Revolted by the purity of white memories, she sank into sensual imagination The warmth of the hearth, the logs still burning, tickled her wickedly; she enjoyed that—she thought that singular kisses were about to descend through the chimney in the form of little angels without wings, hotter and more agile than the capering flames that were playing, agreeable demons, among the embers.

She dreamed about a sumptuous fornication, an unexpected defilement of which she would be the complaisant victim, beside the fire, on that good fur; yes, with the complicity of that good beast, that amiable and devoted goat . . .

The incubus scattered in the lukewarm chamber collected its atoms and materialized . . . A shadow, like an adolescent faun, obscured the mirror on the chimney-breast, and a draught disturbed her hair and warmed the nape of her neck.

She was afraid, but she desired to be even more afraid; however, she dared not turn round or lift her eyes toward the mirror. What she had felt was dolorously soft; what she had seen was disquieting, strange and curiously absurd: a blond and harsh head, with devouring eyes, a large and almost obscene mouth, a pointed beard . . .

She shivered: he must be handsome and tall, very strong, the being that was about to love her! How she would tremble in his arms! But she was already trembling, already possessed, already the prey of the amorous monster that had been lying in wait for her and coveting her.

The fur slid from her shoulders and immediately, a violent kiss stigmatized her bare flesh—yes, a kiss so violent and so ardent that the mark would remain, without a doubt, like that of a red-hot iron. She tried, with the gesture of a woman being undressed, to pull up her mantle and envelop herself with a final modesty, but the Being opposed it, and gripped both her arms with his two hands. That violence did not displease the vanquished woman; she expected it as a tribute; her back and her shoulders were made to be seen, to receive kisses obligingly; was it not their duty as well as their sensuality?

However, the attack accelerated and the panting incubus was blowing like the bellows of a forge, which made her laugh lightly. *How badly he gives himself!* she thought. *He's very awkward . . . I'm going to look at him from the corner of my eye . . .*

As she turned her head, the mask of the beast advanced, and his wide and almost obscene mouth crushed her lips.

She had closed her eyes, but too late; she had seen the monster face to face, and no longer in accordance with the complaisant reflections of a mirror identical to her dream; she had seen him, no longer fashioned by desire but deformed in accordance with the strictest reality: he was so ugly, with his face of a cruel goat, so ugly and so bestial and intoxicated by a determination so precise and so base—that she was indignant, and stood up again.

. . . She saw herself in the large looking-glass at the back of the room, stark naked and all alone in her dismal room.

HYALIS THE BLUE-EYED FAUN

by Albert Samain

THERE was a little faun born in woods of Mycalese battered by the winds, of the commerce of an aegipan and a mortal. Particularities, still slight, denounced the double essence that he divided within him. He did not have the tumultuous and violent strength of the gods of the forest, but his delicate limbs were further withdrawn from the animal sheath; his thighs were covered with hair that was less coarse and bushy; his pointed ears and fine nostrils quivered continually at things; he had pretty gestures; when he smiled, his cheeks hollowed out slightly, and the ingenuousness of his face was then ravishing; but what excited surprise delightfully was the cerulean color of his large eyes, as blue as the sky and the sea, which paraded an astonished gaze around him, mild and distant, like the radiance of the first star that shines in the east when the sun has not yet set.

Brought up by nymphs of the sacred woods, who gave him the name of Hyalis, he did not mix with the young goat-foots of his own age. Their turbulent games displeased him, and he preferred to be alone; then he invented pleasures more in conformity with his nature, and allowed his vagabond curiosity to wander among the plants and animals. Already, obscure presentiments were awakening within him, and before the solemn faces of the world—the Night, Solitude or Silence—a vague emotion gripped him, and a little indecisive soul rose in the pale water of his eyes.

He varied his games incessantly. Sometimes, lying on his stomach in the grass of clearings, he amused himself by watching little insects emerging from the ground, running very rapidly, climbing and descending along slender stems, venturing into the calyx of a flower, suspending themselves at the end of an invisible thread. Sometimes, leaning over a river with clear waters, he contemplated the indolent or abrupt movement of fish, quick to take alarm. Sometimes, having captured a beautiful butterfly, he placed it on the back of his hand and gazed rapturously at the great precious wings, palpitating slowly in the sunlight. Or, choosing a profound spiral seashell, he applied it to his ear, and for entire hours, with a vague smile on his lips, he listened to the sound of the eternal sea in the depths of the enchanted nacre.

At other times, avid for movement, he launched forth, and fatigued himself all day in mad races through the woods and valleys. His greatest joy was to encounter the centaur Capanede, for the latter, seduced by his politeness, always offered to take him with him. Abruptly, he lifted him from the ground, and installed him on this back with a single thrust. Then, knotting his little arms around the powerful torso of the god, Hyalis allowed himself to be carried away. There were long torrential gallops across the plains and mountains; a rude wind struck his face; the trees of the landscape seemed to be running with him; the quadruple sound of hooves resounded on the sonorous earth; a faint fear suspended his heartbeat, and when the rush suddenly stopped, he clapped his hands and laughed in bursts, his eyes shining, his cheeks burning and all his blood intoxicated by distance and speed.

More often, however, a mysterious attraction brought him back to the sea shore. As he emerged from the tenebrous forests or the profound valleys to the sudden revelation of the immense horizon, an inexpressible buoyancy invaded him. So much space entered into his eyes that his soul seemed to him to be enlarged; he drank the air charged with salt avidly, and, pawing the ground with his hooves like a young stallion, he ventured into the waves, shivering.

One evening, when he had lingered on the strand in that fashion, he saw the sirens. It was a warm crepuscular midsummer night. A song rose up from the open sea, strange, irresistible and sad. The air became stifling and heavy, as if it were raining roses in the shadow; the waves stretched silently over the sand; a great frisson passed by, and the entire sea seemed to be dying.

The sirens drew nearer; they advanced as far as the coast, and Hyalis saw their faces at close range. Supernaturally beautiful and pale, they smiled, their faces tipped back in their hair. The pleasure of seeing them surpassed everything he had felt in the world. Slowly, they withdrew with the night; their song weakened, floated in the breeze for a long time yet, and died away. And Hyalis would never forget them.

✳

He grew up, and the secret forces of age drew him closer to the nymphs that populated the surrounding woods. Under the spur of the ancient desire he was stirred by the russet fleeces that shone behind the trees, he pursued the dryads that were laughing in the foliage, and he lay in wait for the plump naiads sprawled on the soft earth around ponds, who suddenly disappeared in a rattle of colliding reeds.

Faithful to his origin, at first he brought a passionate impetuosity to those games; he knew the facile embraces, the ardent mingling of bodies, flesh trodden like autumn grapes in vats; but in such transports only the blood that he obtained from his father was satisfied, and he trailed through those rapid pleasures an anxious and unsated soul.

The nymphs, however, had welcomed him, and more than one strayed in his direction in the evening. Mylitta was the one he sought for preference. He loved her laughter, as clear as spring water, and her light grace, like that of a young fawn. He often brought her seashells, the plumes of rare birds, flowers picked at the very top of a mountain, or gilded honeycombs; and in the warm and odorous afternoon grass he savored the pleasure of her body avidly.

But Mylitta differed little from her sisters. Cheerful and passionate, she abandoned herself to everyone. Hyalis tried to reproach her for it, but he sensed immediately that she did not understand him, and he ceased taking pleasure with her.

At the same time, he acquired a secret distaste for his enjoyments; their monotony weighed upon his heart, and, vaguely anxious, he pined for an unknown caress. Then, sometimes, he was abruptly attracted in his wandering to some heavy rose or violent lily, and crushed his mouth against them recklessly, or he went down to the sea, and from afar, in the nocturnal wind, he respired the sirens.

And he suffered mysteriously in that fashion, for his lips were solitary.

He often went to converse with the sage Glaucos, the old swineherd of the farmer Lycophron; he preferred those grave conversations to the noisy gaiety of the satyrs. Glaucos, who had once possessed great wealth in superb Sidon, had been captured by pirates in the course of one of his long voyages, and nothing remained to him of his former riches. Through his various fortunes he had come to know himself better; charged with days, he amassed wisdom, and inspired words flowed like an unctuous oil over his venerable beard.

He often said to Hyalis:

"My son, I have lived a great deal, and I have learned that the first law of the world is the conformity of beings with their destiny. I often think about you; the soul that gazes through your eyes is not that of a faun, and I fear that some misfortune will overtake you."

"And you, Glaucos, are you happy?"

"I am."

"However, you were not born to be Lycophron's swineherd."

"You can't understand yet, Hyalis. Certainly, I was once rich and powerful, but before anything else, I was born to be free in my thoughts and in my heart, and I was never more so than in this humble condition, where I belong to myself entirely from dawn until dusk."

Glaucos also excelled in recounting the history of gods and heroes, and the little faun never wearied of hearing it. He requested the repetition of the same stories incessantly.

The old man told him about the birth of Apollo in stony Delos; the humorous larcenies of the son in Maia; the descent of Aristaeus into the marvelous coral and emerald grottoes of the domain of the Oceanides; the journeys of Io across Asia; Cypris crowned with violets and borne on golden foam; and the great Dioscures to whom white lambs were sacrificed from the height of the poop, Castor the tamer of horses and the irreproachable Pollux, and their sister, the divine Helen.

He also spoke about the generous earth, dispenser of all wealth, the Ocean, father of things, the return of the seasons, the trees fecund in fruits, the fields, the crops, the flocks, the working of iron and wood, and beautiful cities filled with the murmur of human beings.

Hyalis only understood the old man's words imperfectly. Sitting on the ground at his feet, he interrogated him, and asked him timid questions; Glaucos replied obligingly; stories led to more stories, and the moon often cut out their shadows motionless on the grass of the silent meadows.

A thousand confused thoughts were wakened thus in the mind of the faun, and a pale consciousness arose within his soul like the first light of dawn that skims the silvery crests of the waves.

As he grew older, a more imperious instinct impelled him toward human habitations. When dawn broke he emerged from the woods and went toward the fields, where the sonorous cockerels were responding to one another from one farmstead to the next. At a slow pace he wandered through the cultures that ornamented the earth with regular colors, going along the fields of maize, rye and oats, watching the labor of men from a distance.

Sometimes, slipping as far as the limits of villages, he approached the dwelling of a blacksmith, always resounding with the sound of hammers on the anvil. Above all, he liked to watch horses being shod; on the lifted hoof that was trimmed at first with a chisel, the bare-armed workman applied the red-hot iron with pincers; an acrid odor of burned horn spread through the air, and the anxious horse turned its head.

At other times he paused some distance away from a potter's studio, and he could not take his eyes away from the rapid wheel on which the artisan shaped the formless and docile clay as he wished into harmonious vases.

But nothing equaled his emotion when he penetrated into temples. Those dedicated to Olympians, to Apollo, Diana and Neptune, impressed him particularly. The majesty of the proportions, the nobility of the stones and the sacred silence of the places all invaded him with admiration; and when, advancing into the depths of a deserted sanctuary, where the odor of burned perfumes still floated after sacrifices, he perceived, looming up in the gloom, the image of the Immortal, with a face of marble and eyes of precious stones, stupor struck his limbs, his breast heaved and he sensed the superior soul of the Great Gods descending into his own soul with a magnificent disturbance.

On those days, at the hour when the shadow of trees are elongated and the setting sun invited laborers to un-hitch the oxen, he remained for a long time sitting on a boundary marker, watching the lamps light up in the valley, and it was with an indescribable melancholy that he returned to the forests full of darkness. By night he avoided the clearings where the choirs of goat-foots and satyrs were frolicking, and went rapidly past the grottoes from which lascivious laughter was emerging.

Sometimes, a dryad excited by the famous strange-ness of his azure eyes seized his arm as he passed and drew him toward her. For a moment, the breath of the night, the acrid exhalation of the heavy hair that inun-dated him, and also the obscure counsels of the blood caused him to stop; then, abruptly, he pushed the dryad away, and, as if gripped by shame, he ran to wash away the burning imprint of her fingers on his arm in the nearby spring. Then, quitting the impure marshes and the warm valley depths, he went on to the mountain and advanced to the extreme tip of the promontory that dominated the distant waves.

There, lying in the grass cooled by dew, he tipped his head back.

The night was august on the heights. All around him the dark vault of the firmament was arched; down below, on the sandy beach, the sea brought her waves back and forth with a powerful monotonous murmur; above his head, the innumerable stars scintillated, suspended, as if ready to fall into his eyes. The soul of the maternal earth and those divine skies was confounded with his; a magnanimous ecstasy inflated his breast, and he lived inexpressible hours thus, silent, motionless and intoxicated.

In that epoch, in the fortunate season when the earth is heavy with foliage and flowers, wandering one evening through a wood of sycamores that surrounded the temple of Latona, he perceived behind the florid hedge of a cheerful garden the white Nyza, the cherished daughter of Xylaos, the venerable priest of Apollo.

Standing next to a basin of scaly and green-tinted marble, she was throwing bread to her doves. The tame birds were fluttering around her, seeking the crumbs under her feet, settling on her hand or on her shoulder, and Nyza advanced thus, a vague smile on her lips, in a gentle palpitation of white wings.

Hyalis had stopped abruptly, gripped by the marvel of a beauty that he had not yet suspected. Nyza was clad in a long pale saffron tunic, which, barely elevated by the double swell of her young breasts, fell in straight pleats to her feet shod in blue sandals. Her hair, as blonde as ripening oats, compressed over her forehead by a silver band, ran in even waves along her thin cheeks and swayed over a long, flexible neck. A grace as light and subtle as a perfume was distributed in all her movements; in the fashion she had of lowering her eyelids slowly there was a sacred modesty, and her smile was as suave as a rose.

After having wandered in the garden for some time, and refreshed her languishing flowers with pure water, she went back into the house slowly.

When she had disappeared, Hyalis had the impression that the daylight had suddenly lost all its brightness, and he remained in the same place for a long time, his heart stifled to the point of sadness by a sensation that was too sweet.

The next day, and the following days, he returned to Xylaos' garden, and, hidden in a nearby bush, he kept watch for Nyza's presence.

Almost every day he came to see her; sometimes, sitting next to a basket full of brightly colored Miletus wool she embroidered rich fabrics; sometimes she kneaded sacred cakes, which she perfumed with the red juice of myrtle berries; sometimes she laid out dazzling linen, washed in the river by maidservants, on the fine grass.

On other days—a spectacle, that delighted Hyalis above all—leaning over little Callidice, the daughter of Agathocles, a rich neighboring farmer, she taught her hymns and sacred dances. Holding the child by the hands she made her raise and lower her arms in cadence, deconstructing the complicated interlacement of the steps. Callidice imitated her, not yet skillful. Together they spun, at first slowly, and then more rapidly; the wind lifted up their light tunics behind them, uncovering their tangled feet.

Often Callidice, betraying the measure, stopped too soon or made a false step; then a double laughter filled the garden with its sonorous eruption.

Hyalis never wearied of those gracious tableaux, and he often cursed the passers-by whose approach suddenly forced him to flee.

At first he wanted to keep the secret of his sentiments to himself, but he did not take long to give himself away by means of unconscious confessions; his sudden blushes, his slightly wandering gaze, his excessive skittishness and his unusual gait revealed only too clearly the confusion of his soul, and he spilled his heart around him like a child carrying an over-full vase.

In any case, a secret force impelled him to speak, and he could not help confiding his disturbance to Glaucos.

"My son," said the old man, "I too have known the fever that is agitating you, and the women of Sidon received rich presents from me. Nothing on earth escapes the power of Eros, and his cruelest darts are those he plants in magnanimous hearts. Certainly, I can see that you are on a road full of dangers. Oh, can you not please yourself among your nymphs? Once you talked to me about Mylitta; now, her name never returns to our discourse."

As Hyalis made no response, his eyes fixed on the ground, Glaucos shook his head, and said: "Ah! I see that you scorn them now. Ingrate child, what mortal can give you more joy and show herself as complaisant to your desires? But it's necessary that your destiny be accomplished. You have seen the daughter of Xylaos, and it is by way of amour that you will rise to dolor."

The old man's voice had a solemn tremor as he pronounced those last words, and, taking Hyalis' head between his hands, he made a long and penetrating gaze descend into him and kissed his forehead gravely.

Now Hyalis felt inexplicable sentiments awakening in him every day; a self-consciousness came to him; instead of belonging entirely to shifting and changing impressions of things, he wove between the world and himself the multiple threads of his own thought, perpetually occupied with Nyza, and he lived at the center of himself, like a silkworm in its gilded cocoon.

When he thought about her secretly, a languor flowed into his limbs and penetrated his bones; his soul was glad and his lips smiled spontaneously, as a flower opens.

The smooth water of pools attracted him; he felt an incessant need to reflect his face therein; but at the same time, his own image, faithfully sent back, caused him an indefinable malaise; abruptly he recoiled, and with a violently agitated branch he troubled the mysterious water to the depths.

At the risk of being discovered he multiplied the opportunities to see Nyza's garden; even in her absence, the sight of the places where she spent her life was pleasant.

One evening, when he had ventured thus, he was astonished to find her still there. Standing between the columns of the portico, she was watching the pink moon rise from the depths of the orchard. Her venerable father was sitting next to her on the hereditary marble bench, respiring the cool evening air, his cheek resting on his hand.

Both of them were silent, and no other sound could be heard than the murmur of a fountain and the intermittent cry of a bird.

They remained thus for a long time; the darkness had drowned the garden, and the surroundings took on the solemnity of the shadow.

When the moon, a third of the way through its course, bathed the whole horizon with its soft light, gently, effortlessly, like a boat drifting down a river, Nyza began to sing.

At first her voice was tremulous, uncertain and frail, as if it were about to break; then, gradually, it unfurled in more ample waves, finally to launch forth, vibrant and pure, into the astonished silence of the night.

Fascinated, Hyalis contemplated the young woman. A blue radiance descended over her, and followed her profile with a luminous line; her arms and her neck seemed marmoreal; in her motionless face, only her lips were quivering, and it was as if her eyes, raised toward the sky, were floating in a silver ecstasy. She went down the steps of the threshold and advanced, taking a few steps in the garden.

Hyalis heard the imperceptible noise of the gravel that her tunic dragged as she moved, and every clink that her bracelets made as they played at her wrists resonated in his own heart.

Numb with happiness, he was no longer thinking about anything. Suddenly Nyza, who had reached the limit of the enclosure, perceived the clear-cut shadow of his horns outlined on the ground; at the same time she saw two eyes glinting in the darkness; and, gripped by fear, she uttered a loud scream and fled toward the house.

Hyalis went back, desperate.

He understood now that an abyss separated him from the daughter of Xylaos; all night long he wandered through the thickets. Hands, in the shadows, tore at his heart, and the words of Glaucos, clarified by a strange light, resurfaced in his memory.

He tried to uproot from his soul the thought that was obsessing it, but his efforts were vain, and his ideas returned of their own accord to suffering.

Now he nurtured his chagrin as best he could, exiling himself to the wildest places for preference. There, for entire hours, in a suppliant tone, he called: "Nyza! Nyza!" His voice, more sonorous in the solitude, seemed to multiply his despair, and that illusion, in his distress, was not without charm.

An abandoned lamb, which he had adopted and which he loved tenderly, always accompanied him in his excursions; its light and animate presence—for it incessantly went astray and came back at a run—the familiar grace with which it reached up toward his hand, and its slight frolics, deflected Hyalis from his sorrow momentarily; sometimes, when his heart overflowed with pain, he took it in his arms, hugged it to his breast, pressed his mouth to the little frizzy head with the soft eyes, and felt consoled for an instant.

One day, lying in the russet heather, he was gazing at the distant sea, shining somberly in the sunlight, when the magicienne Ydragone touched him on the shoulder. Ydragone was famous among the pythonesses. By means of her philters she could deflect the course of the stars and cause metals to emigrate, and her enchantments commanded the shades.

"What are you doing here?" she said to him.

"Don't you know, you who know everything?"

"Certainly I know; but Nyza, the daughter of Xylaos, has no suspicion of it."

"Oh, listen," he cried, "and for pity's sake explain to me what I feel; it's like a desire no longer to feel, no longer to see, no longer to think; in sum, no longer to be myself. Tell me, is that not what humans call death? Can you not procure death for me, Ydragone?"

And he raised toward her a lamentable face in which the sunken eyes were burning like embers.

"In truth," she said, "what you request is impossible, for you're not unaware that the blood of the Aegipan flows in your veins, and it's the immortal blood of a god."

"Your philters are so powerful, though," murmured the faun, in a suppliant voice.

"Listen; your pain has moved me to compassion, and I want to try the effect of my enchantments on you. Before then, it's necessary that you bring me something to which you are attached—this lamb, for example."

Hyalis shuddered; the little animal licked his fingers softly.

"I'll bring it to you," he said.

"In addition, Hyalis, know that in order to attack your divine essence, I shall be obliged to employ terrible poisons. You'll suffer horribly."

"What does it matter? I'll come to your abode tonight."

The magicienne's lair was situated in the heart of the mountain.

In the utmost depths of a circle of rocks of monstrous forms, venomous trees were reflected in a heavy and flat water, in shadows that one might have thought eternal. Vipers writhed in the black grass, swarming in knots, and hideous beasts emerged slowly from the pond, splashing in the mud with a dry rattle of scales, agitating multiple hairy feet. An odor of putrescence trailed in the air, and the flame of the torch flickered.

Hyalis advanced in the middle of the night. His face was livid, but his resolute eyes shone with an unusual gleam. As he crossed the threshold of the grotto, a huge bald bird with a human face and a plump pink belly shook two heavy and dirty wings and called him by his name three times.

Hyalis' pallor became frightful, and he stopped, shivering; but Ydragone appeared and he dared not retreat.

"You see," she said to him, showing him a vat from which dense fumes were emerging, "I'm finishing preparing your philter. Have you thought about what I asked of you?"

Without responding, Hyalis held out the lamb. The magicienne took it, extended it over a stone, its head suspended over the vat, and seized a large knife. The lamb was bleating softly, and Hyalis closed his eyes.

Soon, a strange vapor spread, and the entire grotto became red, the magnificent and terrible red of blood.

"Here," said Ydragone, advancing toward the faun; and she presented a cup to him, in which a black liquid was fuming. "Now," she added, "listen to me and fix my words in your mind. When the next moon has accomplished its career in its turn, on that very day, at the same hour as today, you will die. Drink."

Hyalis took the cup, and emptied it. Immediately, he fell backwards, uttering a terrible scream.

It seemed to him that fire had just spread within him, flowing in his veins, biting his fibers, attacking his bones. His limbs contracted, twisting like dry twigs in a flame. He rolled on the ground, tearing shreds of flesh from himself with his fingernails, and clumps of hair. His suffering seemed so atrocious that even Ydragone went pale.

Abruptly he stiffened, and remained motionless; then the magicienne poured a few subtle drops over him.

He opened his eyes again, breathed deeply, and got to his feet.

Like a wood at dawn where the awakened birds make a thousand joyful cries hard at the same time, his soul quivered in every sense, agitated by confused sentiments. He took a few steps blindly; his hands encountered the body of the lamb, and he raised the warm and curly wool to his lips swiftly. Then a strange sensation rose from the depths of his being, like an irresistible wave coming from the open sea and rushing to break on the shore. His breast was inflated one after another by abrupt sighs, and suddenly, from his burning eyes, a mysterious liquid sprang forth, falling in large drops on to his shagreen like a refreshing rain on the dry grass of a meadow. Full of a delectable astonishment, he murmured: "The gods don't know the sweetness of weeping."

From that day on his existence was modified singularly. The thought that he would not bear his pain for much longer attenuated its acuity sensibly.

As a man placed on the bank of a river admires its majestic course more fully than a man swimming in the middle of its flow, so Hyalis, less narrowly linked to the obscure life of the waters and the woods, embraced more amply the order and the laws of the vast universe, and extracted the most profound impressions from his contemplation.

At present, the eternal rhythm of the world, the silent course of the stars, the mobile and infinite sea, the silvery fires of the night succeeding the glare of daylight, the beauty scattered everywhere in beings, from the whinnying of prancing stallions to the delicate flight of swallows, was all filled with a confused rapture.

In addition, Ydragone's poison, continuing its slow progress, attacked his strength dully, and his soul, less nourished by the energies of blood, inclined with a secret sympathy toward the forms of life in which he perceived a decline. The death-throes of a slow dusk, and the fatigue of a flower wilting between his fingers, propagated exquisite frissons over his refined sensibility, and every day he delved deeper into the moving mystery of living with a more nuanced charm.

As he was gazing one evening at a distant funeral cortege, the pallor of the women in their long veils, the dolorous gleam of their eyes, and the bleak slowness of the funeral hymns seized him in a sudden embrace, so deftly poignant that it resembled a sensual thrill, and he said to himself, pensively: "The gods don't know the beauty of death."

More than ever, meanwhile, he thought about the daughter of Xylaos, but his sentiments in that regard were also transformed. The thought that it was because of her that he was about to lose the light, and that he was making the gift of himself thus, illuminated depths within him; and because of that, the regret of quitting the earth and the joy of suffering for Nyza formed a mixture in his heart of a sad and passionate flavor, in which he savored an inexpressible sweetness.

The new moon was on the point of completing its career, and the term assigned by the magicienne had arrived.

As a man departing for a long voyage assembled everything that he needs to take with him, Hyalis spent the day evoking in his memory the most cherished hours; he remembered his puerile days, conversations with Glaucos, the dryads, the great woods and the sea;

insignificant details, resurfacing abruptly in his memory, touched him more than all the rest.

He watched the last dusk falling over the garden of Xylaos, over the orchard bordered by a curtain of poplars with silvery crowns, over the scaly and green-tinted basin where the doves perched before flying up to the roof, over the paths of fine sand, lightly imprinted by Nyza's slender footsteps.

Gradually, things were effaced; the last sounds of the day were more widely spaced out . . .

Night had fallen.

In the distance, the house raised its pale façade and its columns, linked by garlands of foliage. Hyalis climbed over the hedge and advanced into the darkness. The odor of flowers, reanimated by recent rain, was exhaled round him, more penetrating, and at intervals he stopped in order to breathe more deeply.

As he was walking thus, suspending his footfalls cautiously, an object with which his foot collided in the shadow nearly caused him to stumble.

He bent down and recognized a bundle of box-wood twigs that little Callidice had forgotten a little while ago, and he suddenly recalled the delicacies of the child, running around the garden under the nimbly twirled sticks, and her noisy joy when Nyza consented to play with her, making her dance with her, her arms knotted round her waist. That memory of distant hours attained the most tender part of his heart, and he applied the bundle of box-wood sticks, polished by charming hands, to his lips, silently.

He had reached the portico, where the servants were asleep. He stopped, one arm resting on a column, and craned his neck in the darkness. His heart was hammering in his breast and drops of sweat were trickling slowly over his torso and in the hollow of his back.

He listened; turtle-doves nearby began to coo, and then fell silent; the foliage of the garden was stirring with a long murmur.

Then, suppressing the hesitation that was making his knees buckle, he crossed the threshold and groped his way toward a faint light that filtered through closed curtains.

He parted the curtains and leaned forward.

It was Nyza's bedroom. A copper lamp in the form of a bird spread a pale light there. At the back, on a cedar bed incrusted with strips of ivory, the young woman was lying.

Hyalis advanced and studied her. Before that polished forehead, before those eyes sealed by slumber, a supernatural emotion agitated him, and the chamber around him filled with divinity. Then, shivering and pale, he leaned over that face and examined it at close range. A pink and seemingly luminous blood was visible beneath the epidermis; veins traced a blue network over the delicate partition of the temples; a light wisp of hair, which the slightest breath would have caused to tremble, caressed her cheek. Imperceptible tremors passed over the motionless features, like the ripples that a summer breeze propagates of a smooth watery surface; and at times, the furtive shadow of a sensation tugged the lips, brought the eyebrows closer together, and pinched the delicate nostrils.

But what caused Hyalis' heart to melt was the fringed shadow of the long eyelashes over the cheek, and the amber edge of the hair behind the well-sculpted ear, as odorous and mysterious as the forest.

On holding thus beneath his gaze the person he had never approached before, he experienced a sort of vertigo, and immense spaces of thought appeared, succeeding one another within him, like the landscapes dominated by its flight in the eyes of an eagle.

He leaned further forward; a feeble and pure breath passed over his face, and he shivered; it was the respiration of the sleeping young woman.

Her white bosom was rising and falling at regular intervals, and it seemed to Hyalis that he was now united with her, that he was taking a parcel of the divine soul distributed in her body, that he was according the rhythm of his own life with the rhythm of the adored life.

The exquisite mouth was parted in the darkness like a fruit.

Then, impelled by an irresistible desire, he approached his lips to Nyza's lips, as lightly as he could, to the point of touching them, without her waking up, with an almost immaterial contact.

Then he remained still and shut his eyes.

An infinite softness was flowing in his limb; at the same time, it seemed to him that his heart was swelling, becoming vast, splendid and blue, like the firmament of summer nights, and a thousand stars, tracing golden curves in all directions, fell therein.

The moment had come; Ydragone's poison had attained the very sources of his being. An icy chill enveloped him. Like an urn plunged into water, his soul filled rapidly with increasing darkness; he uttered a long sigh, and his head, still suspended by the virgin's breath, slid soundlessly on to the pillow.

Thus died of amour Hyalis of Mycalese, the little faun with the blue eyes.

UNDER THE OLEANDERS

by Catulle Mendès

ONCE, when Duke Theseus was walking with Hippolyta, queen of the Amazons, in a wood near Athens, they saw a young faun under a bush of flowering oleanders on the river bank, who was tickling the nacreous rosy nose of a nymph asleep on the moss with the tip of a perfumed branch.

"Why is that little faun tickling the nose of that sleeping nymph?" asked the Duke.

"Doubtless in order that, having woken up, she can hear him talk about love," said the queen.

But the nymph did not wake up. Her nostrils merely quivered from time to time, under the odorous caress.

The faun decided to employ another means; he made a little basket of his two hands and filled it with flowers, and he allowed all the flowers to fall from a height on to the throat of the sleeping hamadryad. Slowly, with a dreaming arm, the nymph pushed the light burden aside; but she did not wake up.

The faun began to caper around her, rustling the grass, breaking branches; it was like the sound of an entire litter of wolf-cubs quarreling in the undergrowth;

but the nymph was still asleep, her marble-pale bosom rising and falling like a milky tide.

The faun clapped his hands, shouted, sang, imitated the voices of the wild beasts or tender birds that showed their irritation or uttered plaints in the wood near Athens; there were lion's roars that Bottom would have envied, doves' cooings that would have melted Lysander's heart; the nymph remained motionless in sleep, like a lily caught in the snow.

Then, the little faun having begun to weep, Duke Theseus took pity on the infant demigod and drew his gleaming sword, which he had so often resounded on armor in battle; rudely, he struck a nearby rock, which rang terribly in the air; one might have thought that a duel of heroes and gods was racing through the branches, and the echo howled like a wounded warrior! But the eyelids of the hamadryad, a statue fallen in the grass, did not even quiver.

"Someone has hurt her," said the queen of the Amazons.

And she drew nearer to Duke Theseus, and then kissed him, long and ardently, on the lips. At the sound of the kiss, the nymph woke up, and put her charmed arms around the young faun's neck.

THE LAST SATYR

by Théo Varlet

AFTER an abrupt climb, blinded by a thicket, I came out into a dazzling clearing on a terrace emerging from the larch-wood that draped the upper slopes of Mont Antennamare. The lucid panorama of the Ionian and Tyrrhenian Seas presented the convexity of their miniature and supremely still fresco.

Beneath the ultramarine of an Angelico sky, the massive Calabras, dappled with snow, overlooked the peacock-blue estuary, where white Messina enclosed a crop of masts in the antique sickle of its harbor.

To the north, the lapis-lazuli sea widened abruptly, speckled with waves as white as a flock of seagulls, and its colossal slope extended as far as the sharp horizon, where the volcanic cones of the Liparian Islands were frayed at the summit by long streaks of vapor. From Cap Tindarsa, opalized in the distance, to the black clotted waves of the nearby forest, the bare mountains of the Pelorid chain stretched in azure-tinted, glaucous and ashen green planes. Their indolent profiles and bucolic flanks eternalized the sovereign landscape of sensual and divine Trinacria.

Mother of peaceful and luminous voluptuousness, another Greece, lasciviously anadyomene and burned by African suns, displaying on its beaches the nonchalant siesta of its rich cities, a luxurious sister of the spiritual Hellas, the sacred domain of animal deities, where their games, a long time after the death of Great Pan, were still exuberant in the liberty of the dionysiac forest . . . of which I dreamed.

To incite more precise visions, less panoramic syntheses, I sat down on the edge of the rocky terrace, took a copy of Theocritus from my pocket, and started to intone, in Greek, the fifth idyll.[1]

The sonority of the Doric syllables, the familiar spell of the verses, was evoking in the perspectives of my mind the enthusiasm of historic intuitions, when a sound of rustling branches disturbed me.

Brigands?

I started. At that grotesque supposition, however—blunderbusses and pointed hats—I shrugged my shoulders.

"Bah! Some animal."

And I resumed, more attentively than before, rhythmically intoning the verses, which lit up in evanescent imagery.

The noise was indubitable this time—the patter of footsteps, brisk and cautious.

I turned round.

---

1 The poem by Theocritus, the great pioneer of Greek bucolic poetry, which is nowadays known as "Idyll V" features a song contest between the goatherd Comatas and a young shepherd, Lacon, the latter having accused the former of stealing his flute.

A satyr!

More powerful than astonishment, an immeasurable curiosity kept me silent. I stared at the fabulous capriped who was contemplating me, with a suspicious and stupid expression, leaning on a staff.

Old age, the decrepitude of millennia, weighed down upon that survivor of a semi-divine race, the alert and petulant youth of which is commemorated in the marbles of our museums. Extending from his thin goat-like thighs, abundant red hair had invaded his torso and his overly long arms; a gray mane, from which projected chipped horns and scarred ears, hung in wisps over the snub-nosed face, in which a bestial degeneracy had added flesh to the once-anthropoid character—and in the atonal eyes with horizontal pupils there was a vague, confused sadness, the impotent horror of feeling the remaining drops of his ancient divinity drying up in his immortal veins.

We remained mute. To maintain a front, I finally slipped the Theocritus into my jacket pocket.

At that gesture, however, a grimace of infantile dolor twisted the thick slack lips of the silenus.

"No, no Signor! *Ancora!*" he stammered, putting his hairy fingers together and stamping his worn-out hooves.

I obliged his whim, and resumed declaiming the alternate replies of Comatas and Lacon.

A savage bleat cut off the tenth verse. The silenus sobbed, his neck retracted, rolling the green sclerotics of his upturned eyes, whose tears were matting the dense hair of his white beard.

The distraught brute's desolation wrung my heart. I drew closer to the poor lame god and patted him on the shoulder amicably.

He wiped his eyes with the back of his hand and sniffed loudly. An effort of intelligence contracted his pupils, and, with a crooked smile, he spoke, mingling Sicilian and Greek, with pauses and long amnesiac stutters, searching for words.

"Listen, stranger. Your voice has woken me up. I had almost lost my soul, and, as you see, I no longer know the language of my youth. It's my youth that you're reading there—my divine youth—for I'm old, as you see! Old! Old!"

He leaned his chin to his hands, folded over the end of his stick, and he looked at me avidly, with the eyes of a whipped dog, not knowing how to untangle the confusion of his thoughts, knotted by the centuries.

I encouraged him to go on.

Then, assuring his gaze as to my sympathetic attention, he continued.

"Stranger, I shall try to tell you, for you are good, and in spite of your resemblance to the barbarians, the bearers of green umbrellas, who sometimes climb up here, perhaps you are a god. Perhaps you're immortal too?

"Oh, if you knew for how many centuries I have found no one who understands! The people of the region flee at my approach, or throw stones at me. Sometimes, when night falls, I take the risk of going to the farms; the servants mistake me for a smuggler and give me bread and cheese. But if they perceive my horns or touch my hair, they cry: 'To the devil!' and chase me away with pitchforks, and set the dogs on my hooves. I've almost been devoured ten times over. Everyone has forgotten the gods . . .

"Besides which, the gods have deserted Trinacria, or have fallen into ambushes. I believe there are still nymphs, in the town, but I dare not go there; it's an abode of unknown and terrible perils.

"So I remain a miserable, hunted wanderer in the mountains, alone—always alone. I have to spend long, often fruitless, nights lying in cactus hedges with thorns sharper than those of desire, watching out, on the edges of villages, for some peasant woman to pass by . . ."

He broke off, and, in a lower voice, as if for a shameful confidence: "Even that, that last furtive joy, escapes me—for a secret disease is corroding me, a divine malady, which came upon me after a young shepherdess invited me into her cabin one winter night . . ."

And parting his hair bashfully, he showed me his breast and thighs, encrusted with coppery scabs.

"Do you think I can be cured?" he asked, humbly.

"In the town," I said, "there are savant therapies."

"Alas, this disease is sapping the strength that old age had left me. Soon, there will be no pleasure left to me but playing this flute, brought from the town by an obliging goatherd. He even taught me some tunes. Would you like to hear them?"

"Certainly," I acquiesced.

The fellow untangled from his breast, where it hung on a piece of dirty and twisted blue ribbon, a thirteen-sou flute, which he put to his mouth with an assured modesty.

Abomination. "Viens, Poupoule," trembled its hideous refrain, followed by the Cake-Walk, and it was necessary for me to submit to "Tarara-boom-de-ay" before being able to stop the sinister performance, which the poor fallen god whistled frenziedly through his dented tin-plate tube.

"Good, good—have a rest!" I finally exclaimed.

The unfortunate was choking, his lips slate-colored by starvation.

"You're thirsty. Come on, drink!" And I handed him a capacious flask full of a dynamogenic mixture of rum, caffeine and cola.

He swallowed a redoubtable dose. His eyelids fluttered and his eyes lit up. And, inflating his nostrils in a broad bestial and silly smile, he asked: "Is it Nectar?"

"Almost," I said. "Do you feel better?"

Making no reply, he picked up his stick—and, with his spine arched, his hams firm, his hooves rattling on the rock—which sounded hollow—he advanced to a point of the terrace overhanging the vertiginous wooded slope. There sticking his chest out, a sovereign silhouette against the sky, whose light added a gold plush to his ruddy pilosity, with a vigorous sling-shot action, he hurled the staff of his old age, no longer necessary, recklessly into the abyss.

"Hee-ah!" he grunted, wildly, brandishing his fists toward the light. "Hee-ah!" And his thorax swelled, creaking like new leather. "Hee-ah!"

He turned toward me, his expression tumultuous, his lips gleaming, the color of crushed myrtle.

"Yes, Friend, you are a god! Give me the Nectar again!"

He grabbed the flask and gulped a large mouthful; then, snatching the tinplate flute from around his neck, he sent it flying, blue ribbon and all, over his shoulder.

"I remember. I'll make a syrinx. You'll see. How did I forget?"

He was speaking Greek now, in a deep and musical, slightly hoarse voice.

"Let's go!" And he dragged me away, by a path that led away from the end of the terrace, rapidly, imperatively and irresistibly.

We ran over the mountainsides, through the forest. Here and there, lukewarm blue holes cleaved the coolness of the foliage. Then, in the semi-obscurity of tunnels of verdure, a green fluorescence illuminated my companion's pupils. Every time they settled upon me, a spasm of vigor lifted me up; we galloped, frenetically, through the death-traps of that absurd path; we could, by Hercules, have bounded over the tops of the larches and pines.

"You see! I remember. It was before the subversion of the luminous order of things. It was before the stupid Arabs, before the Christians, disparagers of life—in the times that simply were. In the torrid radiance of ancient Sicily, I was a god. In the days of the north wind, drunk on raw sunlight and the heady gusts, I looked down on the waves of the mountains. Their green and voluptuous soul filtered through all the pores of my soul—naked then, and beautiful!—and flowed in my young arteries. The universal heartbeat in my breast. Listen. In the long summer nights, enraptured by the sirocco, I penetrated the essence of the Panic force. Hee-ah! I know again. I'll tell you—on the syrinx."

He fell silent, his hands clutching his pectoral muscles, his head tilted back in the rut of a dionysiac joy, savoring the inexpressible tumult of his enthusiasm, which was induced in me by contagion—me, the resuscitator of a god!

He went on. His somnambulistic feet kicked up pebbles, which rebounded from precipices. His mane became supple and aerated; his fleece, unmatted now, floated like a garment, to the rhythm of his brisk gait, like a rapid dance led by interior harmonies.

We were going down, though. A valley appeared enclosed by undulating crests and girdled with umbrella-pines—and the great bottle-green sloops of the foothills extended down below in terraces of olive-trees, all the way to the red roof of a farmhouse.

Further away, in another sterile ravine, where the mountain was split by hectic landslides, the white threads of the highway appeared in the background. The minuscule bells of an animal flock were tinkling, musical festoons in the silence.

The satyr's ears were pricked, his nostrils flared. He was whistling through his incisors and he seized me by the shoulders, pointing downwards with his hairy index-finger.

"The goats! Do you see them? On the bare back of the mountain, the black goats, like lice."

His breath jerky, trotting nimbly along the granite spur, he drew me toward the herd, which was grazing

the herbage of the impracticable slopes near a bend in
the path.

Abruptly, the capriped let go of me and raced over the
landslides with exorbitant bounds. The little goatherd,
barefoot and clad in goatskin trousers, started to flee
with vain agility, from the satyr's lightning pursuit—but
the dog did not flinch, and the goats, chewing the grass
that was dangling in the beards, watched the aegipan
pass by placidly. He disappeared behind a mass of rocks,
where his victim had just taken refuge.

I galloped around the long bend in the road, breath-
lessly, anguished by the drama that was being perpe-
trated behind the hillock, from which the triumphant
onomatopeias of incoherent hymns soon emerged.

Five minutes later, instead of a catastrophe, I was
amazed to find a bucolic scene: on the knees of the
capriped, the little goatherd, still red-faced from running, was fondling his beard, chattering away, tugging
the two soft and downy appendages at the goatlike
neck—and the enraptured, ticklish god burst out laughing, in the pose of the drunken satyr of Pompeii . . .

But the child, frightened by the sight of me, suddenly, ran off.

Irritated by my stupid anxiety, I called out to the old
aegipan: "Tell me, at least . . ."

"On the syrinx!" he cried. "On the syrinx! Come
on!"

Ten paces further on, he pulled up a bunch of reeds
with a single thrust, of which he chose the best ones.
I handed him my penknife, and, while walking along,

he shaped his pipes, the sonority which he tested as he went.

Then he fixed me with an ironic stare, sniggering in my face, brazenly. "He wasn't afraid of me, you know. He recognized me. You'll see, god-of-the-nectar: I'll tell you—on the syrinx. Eah! I'm still a god! From Drepane to Syracuse, Trinacria was ours. The country folk brought us offerings, and invoked us in their songs.

"On the sloping paths, in the rounded shadows of the umbrella-pines, I sat down with the young shepherds. I taught them new tunes on the flute; and I leaned over, running my fingers through their hair, which had the scent of fresh-cut grass, to see their red lips sliding over the mouthpiece of the pipes, which sometimes cut them and bloodied them with little salty droplets.

"In the long torrid middays of the late summer, when the landscapes quivered fluidly, lying in ambush beside the roads, I waited for the girls coming back from taking drinking-water to the harvesters—and in the ardent silence of the siesta, I caused the shrill cry of transfixed virginities to spurt forth.

"I lay in wait in the green daylight of the forests, at the time when the dainty hamadryads poked their heads out of the trees, cautiously parting their living sheaths of bark and leaping to the ground, supple green nudities. They too were mine.

"And the nymphs, as white and cool as the flesh of nenuphar lilies, who lay back in silence, their eyes closed, on the damp grass, cooing softly, like the gurgling murmur of the nearby stream . . . and then, alone,

I leaned over the spring, to stick out my tongue at my reflection, still grimacing at their dive.

"I went along the edges of forests, sat down beside the sea at sunset, and combed the long hair of my thighs with my fingers, while night fell, sparkling with stars—until the lunar hours of the sirens.

"The sirens are all blue—do you know that? It's swathed in a nacreous squamous fur that they frolic with the fat tritons with lobsters' tails. Poor tritons! But it's naked, in their true azure bodies, that they love one another two by two, the sirens, in moonlit grottoes. Eah! I violated two sirens, stark naked, before the phosphorescent sea, on one equinoctial night.

"I'll tell you, on the syrinx . . ."

All of a sudden, he asked: "Have you any wax?"

"We can buy glue in the town, when we go to see the doctor."

A sudden terror immobilized him.

"No, no! Not the town! I'm cured!"

"As you wish. We'll ask for some wax at a farm."

His excitement was fading away, however; his features crumpled, sweat moistening the thick wrinkles of his forehead. He tottered.

"You're tired," I said. "Have a rest."

The poor god sat down on a patch of pebbles. He crossed his legs and looked at his worn hooves with a sad smile. "What do you think? Do I need to have shoes fitted?"

His head swayed like those of people dozing in a railway carriage. I went to support him, but he stood up, abruptly tensed with grim resolution.

"The Nectar!"

This time, he drank the elixir to the last drop, and then threw the flask into a cactus hedge.

"Now, I'll tell you . . ."

Feverishly adjusting his syrinx, he tried it out—but for want of wax, the pipes came apart.

"So be it, god-of-the-nectar—let's go into the town."

We set off again. He walked with his neck stiff, his head held high, in a somber serenity, beneath the formidable weight of imminent Destiny. His voluble speech confused fragmentary tales, sometimes fulgurating with wild and grotesque visions.

"I was young and agile! I had races with the centaurs through the forests—centaur dung, mixed with pebbles, bouncing, like slingshots of the trunks of holm-oaks and carobs; the centaurs, without stopping, launched their arrows at the red eye of the sun, which peeped, polyphemically, between the eyelids of horizontal clouds—and the gallops of our dionysiac excursions ran all over Trinacria, from one sea to the other.

"I was young, and handsome! The fauns and the sileni . . ."

He became excited, in his stories in which ancient liberty was doubled by that of a satyr—and seeing him, his eyes crazed, dancing and whinnying hysterically, I began to dread the approach of the outskirts of the town, the first houses of which were coming into view.

Evidently, the half-liter of caffeine, rum and cola ingested by the god was putting too much strain on his integral youthfulness, and it was necessary, before anything else, to obtain some antidote from a pharmacist.

I buttoned my own overcoat over my companion's rhedibitory indecency.[1]

"To go into the town," I breathed, and I completed the plausible accoutrement—for a foreigner—with a pocket cap.

We passed through the customs post. The tax-collectors smiled benevolently at the "forester," whom they assumed to be an eccentric Englishman.

I pushed him into a deserted street, drawing him along rapidly.

Suddenly, though, a little girl in a red skirt and corset came around a corner with a bouquet of roses in her hand.

"*Un soldo, Signor, un soldo.*"

It was the catastrophe.

My satyr stopped dead and stopped in front of the little girl, who smiled at him. Then, suddenly, with an "Eah!" of frantic joy, he launched himself forward, snatching the bouquet in his teeth and the terrified girl in both arms.

I ran forward. He bit me, spitting out the roses, struggling—and, intoxicated, furious and epileptic, he escaped, carrying off the little girl, who was screaming loudly.

While, horrified, I left the implausible rape to take its course in the cowardly god's flight, dionysiac in spite of everything, two carabiniers emerged from a side-street, whose skillful trip brought the capriped down.

---

1 Rhedibitory (*rhedibitoire* in French) means "demanding a refund," usually because a product is defective; its use here is eccentrically metaphorical.

It did not take long thereafter. The two avengers of outraged morality disengaged the weeping child and put the handcuffs on her odious abductor. He, heart-broken, decrepit, empty, fallen from the divine centuries—older than tobacco!—looked at me, stupidly and unreproachfully, and looked at the pipes of his syrinx, imperfect forever, scattered on the ground.

And, a ridiculous silhouette, with his flaccid overcoat and the cap dancing on his horns, my poor benighted satyr disappeared, while I repeated to myself the inept, but this time integral, sentence that would record his epitaph the following day, in the local newspapers: "Finally, the filthy satyr was taken to the police station."

THE ISLE OF SATYRS

by Maurice Montegut

MY distant cousin Georges Trédorn died in Senegal three months ago, of a fit of burning fever, it was said aloud, of alcoholic delirium it was said in whispers.

He was a lieutenant in the navy. No one knew the sea better than him. He had a horror of firm ground.

Via the ministry and the consulates the family has received as a heritage three trunks, stained, patched and mottled with labels, which reek simultaneously of seaweed and sandalwood.

Cousin Georges had strange tastes; in all the countries he visited he applied himself to collecting images, sculptures, trinkets and the most . . . natural emblems. He had brought back horrors from Japan. As everyone knows that, it is me who is charged with opening the trunks, making an inventory—and suppressing the indecencies.

And among those vague embalmed things coming from the eighteen points of the world I find yellow papers, steeped in salt, ragged and forgotten, and I read:

＊

Indian Ocean, 15 September

I've returned aboard trembling at what I have seen . . .
I alone have understood . . . my six matelots are brutes
. . . simpletons, at least. I've lost my head . . .

It's necessary, however, that I find it again, that I
write down this nightmare . . . oh, it's frightful! Have
I really seen it? But no, there's no doubt about it, and
it's only up to me to bring back, willingly or by force,
a specimen of those monsters. Barnum would pay me a
million for it; it would be enough to make all the men
in the world vomit.

This is it.

This morning, I was sent on reconnaissance to a group
of previously unknown islands, omitted from the charts.
They're in the open sea, two hundred leagues from any
other land. In a launch, I had my usual six oarsmen. It
was amusing: a map to draw, a sketch to make, and the
Geographical Society in prospect, awarding me a prize
on a day of plenary session next year . . . or another.

I've approached a volcanic soil . . . these islands can't
be very old. It's one of the last sighs of the old planet
that has pushed them there . . . desolate, chaotic country, sparse vegetation, marine flora here and there.

"Heave to!"

A bleak shore, landslides of granite, gray and red.
The water around it is deep.

The largest of the isles is only two leagues around;
this will be quickly done. We enter into that virgin nature . . .

Virgin? Oh!

No trees, no birds, a great blue sky over while soil.

"Dirty little place!" says a matelot.

We advance. Suddenly, we hear bizarre cries, previously unheard, terrifying; and there, racing away at a gallop, twenty paces away from us, is a troop of nameless beings, the rapid vision of which chills . . . and yet, we're bronzed, we seamen.

"Monkeys!" says one.

"No!"

"What, then?"

"Goats!" affirms another.

I keep quiet myself, for what I've seen doesn't resemble anything known . . . except, perhaps, mythological satyrs, and even then with extraordinary variations.

An immense curiosity grips us, and we run after those prodigious animals, those inexplicable phenomena.

The chase is hard . . . the monsters flee recklessly, still crying; and in their howls there are human voices. Finally, by means of surprise, we drive them toward the sea; before the waves they stop, frightened, and face up to us; in a large circle, we draw nearer, also shouting, and, believe me, all very pale.

At a hundred paces I order: "Halt!" and we consider the enigmatic troop. There are twelve, all dissimilar, but all offering a hideous composite of humanity and animality, of goat and human. Some run on all fours, others walk upright. I see one of them that is very tall and hairy, which would be a true goat if it did not have human feet, almost white; but the two most horrible, assuredly, are that goat with a human head and that man with the head of a goat, with inverted horns.

And all of them, terrified by our presence, are weeping, lamenting, moaning and sobbing, with the tones of desperate men, women and children.

An immense frisson traverses my marrows.

I recoiled, my men too.

"Dirty creatures!" said the novice.

As we recoiled, our circle broke, and the twelve creatures, led by the man with the goat's head, passed through our midst and then disappeared into the rocks with caprine bounds, a fantastic agility. It's thus that a bad dream vanishes.

In silence we went around the mass of rocks and returned to the interior. I drew up my maps and traced my sketches, from the top of a hillock, and I gave the signal to depart, in haste to escape the mystery.

In our path, in the granite landslide, there was a cavern. One of my men penetrated into it at hazard; and from a distance I heard him utter a loud "Ah!"

"What is it now?" I responded, dolorously, weary of prodigies.

There was a human skeleton, a real one, on the dry sand of the grotto; it was lying very straight; next to it were a sailor's knife and a hatchet. In one corner, the calcined stones gave evidence of ancient cooking, a makeshift hearth, burning in this desert on cold nights. The man must have died naked; not a scrap of cloth subsists in the vicinity.

Then I had the disgust of understanding. I have reconstituted the shipwreck: the man throwing himself into the sea, naked, like Virginie's matelot,[1] his knife in

____

1 In Bernardin de Saint-Pierre's novel *Paul et Virginie* (1795).

his teeth, a hatchet bound to his waist. Alone on this island, alone with a goat or goats, perhaps arrived from the same ship, perhaps born there, as once were born throughout the earth the archetypes of various races, the primal individuals of living species. And I remembered the crime of bestiality punished by Moses, the monstrous couplings of humans with animals of which legends speak, which poeticize everything.

I had the key to the enigma, and my heart was sickened. A rage gripped me; I wanted to avenge humanity, soiled by that unpunished death, to suppress the evidence of the crime, those hideous human beasts, those demonic products, those creatures of nightmare and folly.

I had the rifles loaded, and again we searched for the ignoble troop. But they were no longer to be found; the horrible creatures had gone to ground, vanished; the isle was silent, nothing was moving there any longer.

Then I thought that bastard creatures, mules and leopards, remain permanently sterile, and I was consoled.

They will not be perpetuated. They have lived, but after them, silence will fall again over their existence, stolen from the laws of nature; and if their bones are ever rediscovered, they will be classified among the prehistorics, the antediluvians, of the epochs lost in the mist and dreams . . .

THE DEATH OF MONSIEUR DE NOUATRE AND MADAME DE FERLINDE

by Henri de Régnier

THE crimson sunset bloodied the large red rose blooming behind the panes of the French windows. The petals were trembling and the thorny branch clawed the crystal. There was a big wind blowing outside, and beneath a black sky, the irritated water of the garden pond was darkening. The old trees were swaying and groaning; the bodies of the trunks threw out the elongation of branches, and suspended the palpitation of leaves. The draught filtered through the joints of the doors. The Marquis, sitting in a large armchair with his elbows on the marble table, was smoking in a leisurely manner. The smoke of his pipe rose vertically until, caught by the eddies of the draught, it swirled, its rings uncoiling in sparse trails. He had gathered the florid flaps of his coat on to his knees. Dusk did not pacify the squall. The large rose moved, clenching the wrath of its thorns. A little bat fluttered back and forth in front of the window, errant and bewildered.

"In order to get back to Ochria," Monsieur d'Amercoeur continued, "it was necessary to take one of two roads. I didn't like the shorter of the two, the sea-road. By the other it was six days on horseback. I made my decision. I had been assured of the bounty of the inns, and the next day, at dawn, I set off over the plain. High ocher-tinted mountains rose up on the horizon; I reached them rapidly. My horse went at a good pace and I let him go.

"The greater part of the journey passed without incident. No encounters, either in the empty hostelries or on the deserted roads. I drew nearer, and on the morning of the sixth day I had only had the remains of the forest to traverse. The place seemed to me to be singularly wild. A landslide of monstrous rocks heaped up broken rumps there, thrust up hairy breasts and extended deformed paws. The stains on the stones imitated the marbling of flesh; pools of water shone like eyes; and the velvet of moss resembled animal fur. The yellow sun hollowed out trails and showed up shiny spurs in places. Reddish pine-needles furred the ground with a russet fleece.

"At the exit from the forest one overlooked a desiccated plain, a landscape of brushwood and hillocks. I paused momentarily to contemplate its monotonous extent, limited by a rocky crest behind which Ochria lay. I was about to set off again when I heard galloping behind me, and a rider mounted on a chestnut horse accosted me, saluting. He was clad in a brown leather hunting costume, which amplified his medium corpulence and stature. His brown hair glittered in places with fawn reflections and his pointed beard reddened slightly. The sun, already in decline, gilded him all over, and the color of his body matched the ocher of the horizon and the gold of the surrounding foliage. He seemed exhausted after a long ride. We went down the rather steep slope side by side.

"Having ascertained that I was going to Ochria, he proposed to go there with me, to take me by the shortest route. The day was coming to an end. We were now moving between emaciated hedges enclosing the aridity of stony fields. At a crossroads we encountered a herd of goats. They were grazing dry grass, their beards were pointed and the movement of their little hooves making their slack udders dance. In their midst, a billy-goat with twisted horns paraded obscenely, pretentious and reeking.

"'He really is the image of an old satyr,' my companion said, with a brief, quavering laugh. He had stopped to consider the beast, which was looking at him curiously.

"The sun was setting. Objects were tinted with pale gold light. The ground we were covering was rank and ingrate, and behind us, the bitter mountain stacked its ocher-striped masses. My interlocutor continued: 'Yes, this land is mysterious and surprising things happen here. Vanished races are remade here; I almost have the proof and am on the lookout for the certainty.'

"Carefully, he took from his saddle-bag a lump of yellow-tinted clay and handed it to me. It crumbled slightly in my hand.

"'Look at that imprint.' He showed me a mark that was almost effaced. 'It's that of a faun. I've also been notified of the presence of a centaur. I've lain in ambush for several nights hoping to catch it. One doesn't see it, but one hears it whinnying. It must be young, its torso thin and its rump still rough. At full moon it comes to look at itself in pools of water, in which it no longer recognizes itself. It's the last survivor of its race—or, rather, its new beginning. The race has been hunted and destroyed, like those of nymphs and satyrs, for they existed.

"'It's said that once, shepherds surprised one in its sleep and took it to proconsul Sulla. Interpreters interrogated it in all known languages. It only replied with a quavering cry, like whinnying. They let it go, for the people of that time still knew a little about truths that have since become obscure. But everything that has existed can be reborn. This land is propitious for the fabulous work. The dry grass has the color of fleeces; the voices of spring murmur ambiguously; these rocks resemble unfinished beasts. Humans and animals live in sufficient proximity for there to be consanguinary exchanges between them.

"'Time has dispersed forms once conjoined. Humans have isolated themselves from their surroundings and withdrawn into their solitary infirmity: a retrograde step taken in the belief that they were perfecting themselves. The gods once mutated themselves into appearances of their choice, adopting the bodies of their desire, eagle or bull! Intermediary beings participated in that divine faculty; it is dormant within us; our passion creates an intermittent satyr there, only incorporating the desires that rear up in us! It's necessary to become what one is; it's necessary for nature to complete itself and rediscover the phases it has lost.'

"My companion talked incessantly and feverishly. I had difficulty following his speech, which he appeared to be continuing without being aware of my presence. In the meantime, the sun had set and, as the darkness became more intense the singular individual seemed gradually to fade away. He lost the russet gleam with which the daylight had impregnated his tanned leather coat, his beard and his hair. His whole appearance deepened; then his excitement calmed, as the landscape changed.

"Soon, we saw the water of a river shining. The moisture that it spread made its banks verdant. A bridge bestrode it with its arches. Night fell rapidly. My companion was no longer talking and I saw his black form beside me, sculpted from the surrounding shadow. When we arrived at the end of the bridge, whose gravel sounded loudly beneath hooves, he stopped abruptly, in front of a lantern hanging from a pole.

"As I looked at him I wondered whether the man who held his hand out to me was really the strange speaker of a little while before. His face seemed different to me, his dark hair and beard no longer ruddy; he appeared slim and elegant and he wore a smile full of politeness when, as he left, he told me his name, in case I might like, during my stay in Ochria to renew my acquaintance with Adalbert de Nouâtre."

The first person that Monsieur d'Amercoeur visited in Ochria was not Monsieur de Nouâtre. Even the memory of that singular individual soon faded from his memory. He gave no thought to renewing his acquaintance and did not run into him. He did not see him while out walking, nor in the taverns, nor at the homes of the courtesans he frequented, to whom access was quickly granted to a young man of his name, well-equipped with horses, clothes and jewels. Two of the most lustful fought over him determinedly. One was brunette, and stole him from the other, who was blonde, and who took him back, although he found it easier to satisfy them both by turns than choose between them.

His appetite for debauchery and gambling rapidly associated him with the most elegant young people in the town. He was soon invited to all the parties. He enjoyed himself there and, as graybeards love to get mixed up in the disorders of youth, came to make the acquaintance there, through the intermediary of the pleasures everyone sought, with many serious individuals whom it would otherwise have been difficult for him to meet.

That commerce established him squarely in the best society in Ochria. After meeting him so frequently in their mistresses' houses, those gentlemen went on to introduce him to their wives, and Monsieur d'Amercoeur was soon familiar with the large silent houses at the back of their paved courtyards. He sat down at sumptuous tables, savored the dishes of knowledgeable cooks, drank wine from centuries-old cellars and saw the important personages and beauties of the city paraded in their finery beneath crystal chandeliers.

He found one among them particularly seductive. Her name was Madame de Ferlinde. She was slim and red-haired. Her long supple body supported a pagan head, crowned with tresses whose wavy cascade concluded in spirals. The incandescent mass of that hair seemed both fluid and sculpted, with the boldness of a helmet and the grace of a spring. She had the attitude and the bearing of a warrior Nymph. A widow, she lived in an old house amid beautiful gardens. Monsieur d'Amercoeur was soon going there assiduously, spending whole days there, arriving at all hours without the shepherd's hour ever chiming for him.[1]

That chaste Diana loved to adorn her beauty with creased tunics and lunar crescents, and merited the name of the goddess. She loved invisible orchestras, the shadow of love and the murmur of water. Three fountains gushed harmoniously in the midst of an arbor. The garden also contained a little grotto in which Madame de Ferlande often came to rest. Hanging ivy veiled it from the sunlight, creating a pale green light within.

It was there that she first talked to Monsieur d'Amercoeur about Monsieur de Nouâtre. She depicted him as a man of manias, but erudite and charming, with a prodigious knowledge and refined tastes, who led a solitary life, frequently absent on travels, a great collector of books, medals and engraved stones.

---

1 *L'heure de berger* [the shepherd's hour] is a euphemism employed to indicate the fulfilling moment of a lovers' rendezvous.

Without revealing the details of his meeting with Monsieur Nouâtre, Monsieur d'Amercoeur spoke about it as an occasion when the latter had been very obliging, and accepted from Madame de Ferlinde the offer she made to visit him together, so that he could thank his traveling companion and she could see a friend who had neglected her for some time. On the agreed day, they therefore went to Monsieur de Nouâtre's home.

As soon as they went in, they saw an antique bronze in the middle of the vestibule representing a centaur. The broad torso was bulging with muscles, the rounded hindquarters gleaming; the flanks seemed to be palpitating; the raised hoof was at the ready, and the equestrian monster was raising an onyx pine-cone above his vine-clad head.

Everywhere their host took them, Monsieur Amercoeur admired an exclusive choice of objects concerning the history of terrestrial or marine demigods and the magical mythology of the ancients. Their effigies were modeled in earthenware, their legends evoked by bas-reliefs, their cults rememorized on medallions. Harpies with sharp claws, poisonous or winged Sirens, club-footed Empusas,[1] Tritons, Centaurs—each of them had a figurine or statue there. The bookcases contained texts relating to their origin, their existence and their nature. There were treatises on their species and their forms, enumerating all the kinds of Satyrs, Sylvans or Fauns,

---

1 The Empusas of Greek mythology were malevolent female spirits that supposedly lured male travelers from beaten tracks and drank their blood; they were akin to lamias, but generally considered to be uglier, often one-legged or limping.

and one of them—the rarest, which Monsieur Nouâtre displayed with a certain pride—contained a description of the Papposilenus,[1] which is a horrible monster entirely covered in hair. Manuscripts in admirable bindings, retained the recipes for the Thessalian philters by means of which the witches of Lucian and Apuleius changed humans into owls or into donkeys.[2]

Monsieur de Nouâtre showed off his collection marvelously. Sometimes, a slight smile stretched his mouth. In his exceedingly dark eyes, coppery streaks scintillated at times, and three golden threads glinted in his brown beard. When they parted, he squeezed Madame de Ferlinde's hand between his sharp-nailed fingers, and while he looked at her, Monsieur d'Amercoeur saw metallic yellow gleams multiplying in his eyes, like a kind of furtive lightning, impassioned and violent, which vanished almost immediately.

That first visit did not remain unrepeated. Monsieur d'Amercoeur often revisited the stucco vestibule where the bronze Centaur stood, hoof upraised, on its marble pedestal, the onyx cone shining in its hand. Monsieur de Nouâtre never explained the origin or the objective of the singular collections assembled in his house. He only

---

1 *Papposilene* [Papposilenus] is a rare pleonasm, in that sileni are already, by definition, aged satyrs, and adding the prefix *pappo* [old] is therefore redundant. The author evidently feels that the reinforcement is functional in this case, in order to suggest a further level of exaggeration to the existing image of the satyr or silenus.
2 Apuleius' Latin proto-novel *Metamorphoses*, better known as *The Golden Ass*, describes the extravagant exploits of a witch named Pamphile; it appears to have been based on an earlier prose satire in Greek attributed to Lucian, most commonly known as "The Ass."

talked about them in order to comment on the rarity of a book or the beauty of a trinket. Neither did he make any allusion to the circumstances of their first meeting. His reserve was matched by Monsieur d'Amercoeur. Their relationship of ceremonious amity kept the secret of the former and did not authorize the curiosity of the latter, and they both seemed to be in agreement in feigning a reciprocal forgetfulness.

"Madame de Ferlinde had been anxious for some days when she asked me to come to see her. I responded to her appeal and found her nervous and preoccupied. When I pressed her to tell me the cause of her disturbance, she replied evasively, but ended up confessing the singular apprehension in which she was living.

"She told me that the dogs howled every night, more out of fear than anger. The gardeners had discovered traces of footprints on the sand of the pathways. The grass, trampled in places, revealed a nocturnal presence—and to my great astonishment, she showed me a clod of earth on which a bizarre imprint could be seen. It was a rather clear impression. On examining the hardened print at closer range I perceived a few yellow hairs embedded in the clay.

"An invisible marauder seemed to be haunting the garden and spying on the house. Traps had been set in vain, and nocturnal patrols were being undertaken. In spite of everything, Madame de Ferlinde could not help feeling an insurmountable apprehension. I did the best I could to calm the fearful beauty and, on quitting her, promised to return the following day.

"It was late Autumn; it had been raining; the streets were still muddy, the trees losing their leaves, red and yellow in the twilight. The main gate was open, the gate-keeper asleep in his lodge. I went into the vestibule and waited for a valet who could announce me to Madame de Ferlande. Her bedroom, which overlooked the garden, was at the end of a corridor. I waited for some time. There was no movement in the vast silent dwelling. No one came, and time passed.

"A faint noise reached my ears; I listened more attentively and it seemed to me that I heard muffled sighs, and then the fall of an item of furniture that had been knocked over. I hesitated; there was total silence. Suddenly, there was a heart-rending scream from Madame de Ferlinde's bedroom. I ran along the corridor and crashed into the door, which opened wide.

"It was already dark, but this is what I glimpsed: Madame de Ferlinde was lying on the parquet, half-naked. Her hair spread out is a long golden stream; and crouching on her breast was a kind of hairy beast, deformed and spiteful, embracing her and devouring her with its lips.

"As I approached, the mass of yellow hair bounded backwards. I heard its teeth grinding and its nails scraping the parquet. An odor of leather and horn mingled with the sweet perfume of the room. Sword in hand, I rushed upon the monster. It spun around, overturning the furniture, clawing the wall-hangings, evading my pursuit with an incredible agility. I tried to trap it in a corner.

"Finally, I made contact with its abdomen; blood splashed my hand. The brute sank back into the dark corner and then, with a sudden bound, knocked me over, leapt out of the open window into the garden, to the sound of breaking glass.

"I went to Madame de Ferlinde; warm blood was running from her torn throat. I lifted up her hand, which fell back limply. I listened to her heart, which was no longer beating. Then I was gripped by panic; I fled. The vestibule was still empty, the house seemed mysteriously abandoned. I went past the sleeping gatekeeper again. He was snoring with his mouth open, in the inertia of a lethargy that subsequently seemed suspicious, as did the absence of any servant in that isolated house, where Madame de Ferlinde appeared to have sensed something bestial prowling in ambush around her beauty.

"It was dark. I wandered the streets in an inexpressible disorder. Rain began to fall. That lasted for some time. I was still unconscious of where I was when, raising my eyes, I recognized Monsieur de Nouâtre's house. I knew that he was a friend of the chief of police and the idea came to me of consulting him, and of informing him of the tragic event of that frightful night. Given the unexpectedly deserted house and the sequence of inexplicable facts, my presence at the scene of the crime constituted a monstrous accusation against me, of which it was urgently necessary to divert any suspicion.

"I rang. A domestic told me that Monsieur de Nouâtre was in his bedroom, to which he had been confined for several weeks. I went upstairs precipitately. A clock chimed eleven. I knocked and went in without waiting for an answer—and stopped on the threshold.

"Darkness filled the vast room. The window must have been open, because I could hear rain outside on the deserted street that the house overlooked at the rear. I called out to Monsieur de Nouâtre. No reply. I went forward into the shadows, hesitantly. A few embers were glowing in the fireplace. I lit a torch therefrom that I had found on a table with which my hand had collided. The flame sputtered.

"A body was lying face down, extended on the parquet. I turned it over and recognized Monsieur de Nouâtre. His wide-open eyes gazed at me vitreously, like unpolished onyx. There was pink foam at the corners of his lips. When I felt his hand it filled mine with blood. I parted the black cloak that enveloped the cadaver. There was a deep wound in the abdomen, made by a sword-thrust.

"I felt no terror; I was gripped by a violent curiosity. I looked around attentively. Everything in the bedroom was in order. The white curtains of the bed were open. There were muddy footprints on the polished diamond-patterned parquet; they extended from the window to the spot where Monsieur de Nouâtre lay. A bizarre odor of leather and horn infected the air. The fire crackled; two adjacent brands reignited, and I then perceived that the wretch had fallen with his feet in the fireplace, and that the flame had burned his shoes and charred his flesh.

"That double death caused great excitement in Ochria. I was summoned to the high court, but no one challenged me on the statements that I made. The connection of the tragic facts remained forever doubtful, and in suspense. Madame de Ferlinde left no heirs and her wealth reverted to the poor, along with that of Monsieur de Nouâtre, who was similarly devoid of family, although he had made a will in which he left me, in memory of him, the bronze Centaur ornamenting his vestibule, holding an onyx pine-cone in its hand."

The valet came limping in and, one by one, lit the candles in the brackets and those of a large candelabra, which he placed on the table. Then he opened the French windows in order to close the external shutters. The wind was still blowing; an odor of roses and box came from outside and, attracted by the light, a little bat flew into the vast room. It flew around the ceiling as if it were trying to draw a circle there, incessantly recommenced and broken every time by an abrupt deflection. Its delicate wings were beating rapidly.

The Marquis remained huddled in his embroidered silk dressing-gown, and we watched the agile beast patiently persisting in its mysterious task, interrupted by the hitches of its haste and spoiled by the captious meanders of the inextricable thread of its flight, signing the air with the magical flourish of its intermittent incantation.

THE DOORS OF SAINT-MACLOU

by Maurice Leblanc

T HE catechism ended. The flood of children flowed away through the aisles with a buzz of joyful voices and the click of shoes on the sonorous paving stones. The holy water fonts were assailed.

In the middle, along the nave, Abbé Bouache descended, escorted by a group of parents, good sisters and brothers of Christian schools. In an angry tone he lamented the ignorance and vicious nature of his pupils. His gestures trembled with indignation and, starting on his favorite thesis, he launched a direct attacked on the parish of Saint-Maclou in the Martainville quarter,[1] where all the poverty and all the shame of Rouen came together, that hearth of debauchery where criminals, drunkards and loose women—the foolish virgins of whom the Gospel speaks—were formed.

He seemed to be preaching, sometimes pausing, opening his arms in broad oratory movements, his

---

1 The fifteenth-century Church of Sant-Maclou in Rouen is one of the best examples of the "flamboyant" school of Gothic architecture to be found in France. The portal sculpted by Jean Goujon can still be seen, as can the satyrs' heads he sculpted on the keystones of the arcade in the courtyard.

eyes creased by a grim ardor. The group were silent, frightened.

They arrived at the exit, a kind of obscure chamber adjacent to the main door. Abbé Bouache introduced himself into it. In the darkness children were crouched, examining curiously by the light of a match the inferior part of one of the two battens.

They did not hear him. Then he too leaned over. And suddenly, a hoarse roar escaped him, he leapt upon the boys, jostling them, striking left and right. And as they fled he pursued them through the porch all the way to the neighboring streets. Passers-by gathered.

He came back through the sacristy. The church was almost dark. He knelt down on the steps of the altar. His head was on fire. He tried to pray but could not succeed. Ideas besieged him, innumerable and dolorous. One above all became precise in a terrifying image, the reality of which punctured his eyes. A hope, however, occurred to him. Who could tell? In the darkness, an error is possible.

The stub of a candle was standing next to him. He lit it, and ran to the entrance, toward the famous doors, attributed to Jean Goujon.

The batten before which he stopped is divided by a bronze handle into two parts. The superior subject symbolizes Christianity, a man marked on the front of a cross. The other, below, represents two cupids playing at the foot of a tree, with, to either side, leaning on the branches of the medallion, two satyrs.

The abbé stuck the light to them. Alas, he could not doubt it; it was human nudity, brutal and obscene nudity.

The certainty, this time, made his legs weaken. He collapsed. The candle went out. And he remained there, stupefied and bewildered. Something was triggered within him that prevented any revolt. The love of priests for their parish, for the church that they consider to be their own, as a living and cherished thing, the respect and the pious tenderness that once had penetrated him, all drained away. What sacrilege! The idol was soiled, unworthy in consequence of his veneration. Soiled, the altar at which he celebrated the divine sacrifice every day! Soiled, the high nave into which his voice, vibrant with adoration, launched the Christian *Pater Noster*! All soiled, the Virgin, Saint Joseph, the saints of the chapels, all, everything, seemed to him to be soiled, including God himself!

From then on, existence was intolerable to him.

He was a tall, thin man, with automatic gestures, like a mannequin decked out in a soutane. His soul, like his body, was narrow and stiff. Only his eyes were alive, the eyes of an inspired individual, a soldier yearning to die for the good cause.

Far from seconding him, however, that ardor did him a disservice. His excessively rigorous virtue had forbidden him access to the posts that his more flexible colleagues attained. In his successive parishes, his neophyte zeal, his need to command and impose his God, had alienated him from the peasants. And he wandered from village to village, always at odds with the maire or with the faithful, squabbling with the church council, suspicious of the archbishop.

Finally, after ten years, he had been sent to Rouen as the third priest of Saint-Maclou. That post pleased him, that quarter of poverty and impiety suited his battling nature. He attempted conversions. Devout old women held him in high esteem. He badgered workers even in their taverns.

The discovery of the infamous sculpture abolished every vestige of those joys. He could only think about that, could only see that. In vain, when he crossed the threshold of the church, he closed his eyes in order not to dirty them with the hideous vision; in the midst of the vague and changing images that danced behind his closed eyelids, the two satyrs loomed up, immobile and precise, superb with desire. They were engraved in his brain. They ran before him with their hairy legs, they hugged him with their wiry arms, they mingled with the things he touched, took on the appearance of the things at which he gazed.

One day, mad with terror, he threw away the host, attributing to it, in his hallucination, he knew not what strange form.

He was no longer able to pray. He officiated mechanically. His sermons seemed to be lessons pronounced at random. He was prey to a single idea, like a monster weighing upon him, resident within him, poisoning his blood, vitiating his dreams.

Other tortures lacerated him. Did not the same obsession attain those who frequented the church? He accosted visitors, gave the explanations of the stained-glass windows or the staircase to the organ loft, denigrating the value of the two doors, "which are apocryphal," he said, and tried to draw them away without them having seen the medallion of the two satyrs.

His parishioners worried him most of all. He kept watch on them, hidden behind a pillar. Sometimes he slid all the way to the cage, opened it and advanced his head precipitately. When children arrived for the catechism and when they left he placed himself in their passage, and his broad soutane hid the bas-relief. In the confessional he integrated his penitents minutely, distinguishing in every sin an unadmitted and perhaps graver motive, always the mark of lust that profaned the church.

He did not admit that other causes might engender sin; for *that* is the commencement of everything, *that* dominates us, commands us, maddens us, *that* is the emblem of amour, the symbol of the union of bodies; it is the original sin, the great din that doomed us all and will doom us all. And *that*, O shame, the germ of mortal soiling, was displayed in the house of God. God himself was propagating the evil. It emanated from him like a contagion. The gangrene had its point of departure, its hearth, in the house of the very person who forbids succumbing to it. And he saw God floating above the world, leaning toward him, and, like a gigantic sower, pouring with both hands vice, appetites, concupiscence and amour, all the sins that he punishes with Hell!

And he too was shaken by dreams of lust, and he had culpable desires for women who passed by.

Fear took hold of him. He sensed that he was vanquished. The two satyrs wanted his fall. Their presence had corrupted the faithful, they now required the ignominy of the pastor. What was the point of struggling?

He was suffering so much that all his energy was dissipated, and he waited, resigned in advance to debauchery and turpitude.

Then, suddenly, a glimmer of light, an absurd project illuminated his brain. That project, he welcomed instantaneously with an ardent joy. No other means was offered to him. There lay his salvation.

He did not defer fulfilling his duty. Two or three times he lurked under the porch and considered his enemies, no longer cursing them tremulously, as before, but as a calm, resolute, pitiless adversary, sure of his triumph.

And one night, equipped with a hammer and chisel, he went into the deserted church and marched toward the two satyrs.

The affair made a great deal of noise. The municipal council protested against such an outrage. Abbé Bouache, who proclaimed loudly his responsibility for the mutilation, was dismissed.

But the episcopal authority had eyes upon him. Such an energetic character, such a keen piety, a soul that evil wounded so profoundly, merited being distinguished. He obtained a rapid advancement.

AMYCUS AND CÉLESTIN

by Anatole France

PROSTRATE on the threshold of his grotto, the hermit Célestin was spending in prayer his Easter vigil, on the angelic night when the shuddering demons were precipitated into the abyss. And while the shadows covered the earth, at the hour when the exterminating angel had soared over Egypt, Célestin shivered, gripped by anguish and anxiety. In the distance, in the forest, he could hear the mewling of wild cats and the fluty voices of toads; plunged in the impure darkness, he doubted that the glorious mystery could be accomplished. But when he saw the day break, delight entered his soul with the dawn; he knew that Christ was resuscitated and he cried:

"Jesus has emerged from the tomb! Love has vanquished death, Alleluia! He is rising up radiant from the foot of the hill, Alleluia! Creation is remade and repaired. The shadow and evil are dissipated; grace and light are spreading over the world, Alleluia!"

A lark that had woken up in the wheat responded to him in song.

And the hermit Célestin emerged from his grotto in order to go to the nearby chapel and solemnize the holy day of Easter.

As he was going through the forest he saw a beautiful beech tree in the middle of a clearing, the swollen buds of which were already allowing little tender green leaves to escape. Garlands of ivy and hanks of wool were suspended from the branches, which hung down all the way to the ground. Votive tablets attached to the gnarled trunk spoke of youth and amour, and here and there, clay effigies of Eros, his wings open and his tunic flying, swayed in the branches. At that sight, the hermit Célestin's white eyebrows frowned.

"That's the tree of the fays," he said to himself, "and the young women of the region have charged it with offerings, in accordance with ancient custom. My life is spent struggling against the fays, and no one can imagine the trouble those little folk give me. They don't resist me overtly. Every year, at harvest time, I exorcize the tree in accordance with the rites, and I sing them the Gospel of Saint John.

"One can't do any better; the holy water and the Gospel of Saint John put them to flight, and no more mention of those ladies is heard all winter, but they come back in the spring and recommence every year.

"They're subtle; it only requires a hawthorn bush to shelter a whole swarm. And they cast spells on the young men and the young women.

"Since I've grown old, my sight has deteriorated and I can scarcely perceive them any more. They make fun of me, thumbing their noses at me and laughing at my beard. But when I was twenty I saw them in the clearings, dancing rounds in flower hats in the moonlight. Lord God, who made the sky and the dew, be praised in your works! But why have you made pagan trees and magical springs? Why have you put under the hazel tree the mandrake that sings? Those natural things induce youth to sin and cause fatigues without number to anchorites like me, who have undertaken to sanctify creatures. If only the Gospel of Saint John were still sufficient to expel demons! But it isn't sufficient, and I no longer know what to do."

And as the good hermit drew away, sighing, the tree, which was enchanted, said to him in a fresh rustle: "Célestin, Célestin, my buds are eggs, true Easter eggs! Aleluia! Alleluia!"

Célestin plunged into the wood without turning his head. He was advancing with difficulty along a narrow path, in the midst of thorns that tore his robe, when a young boy bounding from a bush barred his way. He was half-clad in an animal skin, and was a faun rather than a boy; his gaze was piercing, his nose snub, his face laughing. His curly hair hid two little horns on his stubborn head; his lips uncovered sharp white teeth; blond hair descended from his chin in two points. A golden down shone on his breast. He was agile and svelte; his cloven feet were dissimulated in the grass.

Célestin, who possessed all the knowledge that meditation gives, saw immediately what he was dealing with and he raised his arm in order to describe the sign of the cross; but the faun, seizing his hand, prevented him from completing that powerful gesture.

"Good hermit," he said to him, "don't exorcize me. For me, as for you, today is a feast day. It would not be charitable to sadden me at Easter. If you wish, we can walk together, and you'll see that I'm not wicked."

Fortunately, Célestin was well versed in the sacred sciences. He remembered appropriately that Saint Jerome had had satyrs and centaurs for traveling companions in the desert, who had confessed the truth.

He said to the faun: "Faun, be a hymn of God. Say: he is resuscitated."

"He is resuscitated," replied the faun, "and you see me full of joy."

The path had broadened, and they were walking side by side. The hermit was pensive and thought: *He isn't a demon since he's confessed the truth. I did well not to sadden him. The example of the great Saint Jerome has not been wasted on me.*

Turning to his companion, he asked him: "What is your name?"

"My name is Amycus," the faun replied. "I live in these woods, where I was born. I came to you, Father, because you have a rather benevolent air under the long white beard. It seems to me that hermits are fauns overwhelmed by the years. When I'm old, I will be like you."

"He is resuscitated," said the hermit.

"He is resuscitated," said Amycus.

And, conversing thus, they climbed the hill where a chapel stood, consecrated to the true God. It was small and primitive in structure; Célestin had built it with his own hands with the debris of a temple of Venus. Inside, the Lord's table was deformed and bare.

"Let's kneel down," said the hermit, "and sing Alleluia, for he is resuscitated. And you, obscure creature, remain on your knees while I offer the sacrifice."

But the faun, drawing nearer to the hermit, caressed his beard and said: "Good old man, you are more knowledgeable than me, and you see the invisible; but I know the woods and the springs better than you do. I have brought the good foliage and flowers. I know the banks where the water-cress opens its lilac corymbs, the meadows where the cowslip flowers in yellow clusters. I divine by its odor the mistletoe of the wild apple tree. Already, a flowery snow is crowning the blackthorn bushes. Wait for me, old man."

In three caprine bounds he was in the wood, and when he came back, Célestin thought he was seeing a walking hawthorn bush. Amycus disappeared beneath his perfumed harvest. He suspended garlands of flowers from the rustic altar; he covered it with violets and said, gravely: "These flowers are for the god who gave them birth!"

And while Célestin celebrated the sacrifice of the mass, the capriped, bowing his horned head all the way to the ground, adored the sun and said: "The earth is a great egg, which you fecundate, sun, sacred sun!"

From that day on, Célestin and Amycus lived together. In spite of all his efforts, the hermit never succeeded in enabling the half-human to understand the ineffable mysteries, but, by virtue of the cares of Amycus, the chapel of the true God was always ornamented with garlands, and more florid than the tree of the fays, so the holy priest said; "The faun is a hymn of God."

That is why he gave him holy baptism.

On the hill where Célestin had constructed the narrow chapel that Amycus ornamented with flowers from the mountains, woods and streams, a church stands today, the nave of which dates back to the eleventh century and the porch of which was re-edified under Henri II in the style of the Renaissance. It is a place of pilgrimage, and the faithful venerate there the blessed memory of Saints Amic and Célestin.

THE LITTLE FAUN

by Catulle Mendès

A T the bend in the path, on his terracotta pedestal, the little faun was laughing boldly. Horned, swollen-cheeked and pot-bellied, he laughed, the lubricious, naked young god—being the one who presided over the fluttering couplings of sparrows in the sand, the crepitant caresses of dragonflies over the heather, the rapid and fleeting marriages of squirrels along the branches. But it was not sufficient for his triumph to show that bestial joy. Brazen to the point of cynicism, disdainful of all modesty, like a drunken Eros, he affirmed in broad daylight, like a sign of supremacy, his arrogant virility, like a young king holding the scepter of command. With the result that the faun in question was an object of scandal for the honest passers-by, and that many strollers could not see him without blushing beneath their eyelashes or concealing a little laugh behind the rosy trellis of their interlaced fingers.

But Berthe-Marie, the demoiselle of the château, charitable and devoted, so good and so pure, who went every day to the church where people pray and the cottages where alms are distributed, passed by without blushing or averting her eyes from the bold simulacrum; she considered it, smiling, with a complacency that was slightly astonishing but not at all fearful, in the peace of an inviolate innocence, neither pensive nor anxious, the depths of her blue eyes reflecting the perfect ingenuousness of a child taking pleasure in looking closely at the pictures in a missal, and touching them with her fingertips. For she was candor itself, ineffably ignorant of evil; and if lakes of immaculate azure exist on some Alpine plateau, which have never even been traversed by the shadow of a white cloud, it is one of those lakes that her soul resembled.

One morning, she went into the woods with her lover, who was her fiancé. Yes, with her lover. Why not? Virgin hearts have their affections too; one can give oneself without giving oneself, and a betrothal ring is not the ring of Hans Carvel.[1]

He was almost as young as her, they were as naïve and tremulous as one another; it was to be an exquisite day! They did not hold hands, were careful not to allow their elbows to touch, both aware as if by instinct of their sensitivity. But their souls were united in spite of their bodily separation.

---

1 The story of Hans Carvel seems to have been first committed to print in a collection of lewd tales, *Liber Facietarum*, assembled by the papal secretary Poggio Bracciolini (1380-1459); it was retold by Rabelais and then recast a fable in verse by Jean de la Fontaine. Carvel, an old doctor with a young wife, dreams that the devil gives him a ring that will prevent him from being cuckolded as long as he wears it. When he wakes up he finds that his finger is stuck in her vagina, with the result that "Hans Carvel's ring" became a common euphemism for that anatomical feature.

Wordlessly, they exchanged thoughts in immaterial conversation, the alternating distichs of an angelic eclogue. It was in vain that around them, in the sunlit air where ardent odors were vaporized, branches brushed one another with gentle caresses, and flying green-gold beetles traced redoubtable magic circles, and the voice of the nightingale faded away, ecstatically, beside its nest, and that the entire wood, full of love, enveloped them, gave them the culpable advice of embraces and united lips; they went through the perils, without paying any heed to such sweet wicked temptations.

Not once—not once!—did he press her to his heart, not once did they look at one another too closely, sighing. They were, in that paradise which they did not want to lose, like an Eve and an Adam who were not thinking about forbidden fruit. Yes, such would be, all day long, the slow excursion beneath the trees of those two pure children, and I would even swear that they would not linger to search in the moss for the little fresh strawberries that are reminiscent of kisses, nor to interrogate the daisies, those providers of troubling answers.

It was after dark, in the moonlight, when they returned. Certainly, in the depths of her large blue eyes, Berthe-Marie still had—and why should she no longer have had?—the ingenuousness of ineffable ignorance . . .

When they passed before the faun, horned, swollen-cheeked and pot-bellied, who was even more boldly triumphant, the lubricious little god, like a young king holding the scepter of command, she turned her head very swiftly, and started to laugh, stifling her laughter in her friend's neck.

GABRIELLE AND HER FAUN

by Frédéric Boutet

GABRIELLE'S FATHER was unknown and her mother was a laundress. As the latter destined her daughter for great things—a dressmaker in the Rue de la Paix, or perhaps a pupil at the Conservatoire—she did not torment her at all, save for a half-hearted and perpetually-deferred threat to make her take piano lessons. In the meantime, she spoiled her as much as she could and let her do whatever she wanted. Gabrielle, who was called Gaby, was one of those fortunate individuals who pleased everyone, and whom everyone strove to please. She was, moreover, a good little girl who spent her childhood either wandering the streets or sitting under the big ironing table in her mother's shop, listening, with a desire to educate herself, to the dirty talk of the washerwomen, which she only understood incompletely, but much more than was believed.

Her mother sent her to school regularly, and she went willingly, when the weather was not too fine. The teacher was an old lady with a few qualifications; Gabrielle was her favorite, to the extent that she kept her close during class in order to give her lumps of chewing-gum and tell her long marvelous stories. In these tales, which the old lady made up according to the inspiration of the moment, at hazard, the heroes and events of real history were mingled pell-mell with fairy tales, Biblical traditions and mythological legends, one story leading to another—to the greater delight of Gabrielle, who had imagination. She reveled delightedly in the superhuman adventures, the hybrid monsters, half-human and half-beast, and the fabulous heroes who had such sublime adventures.

And young Gaby spent considerable number of hours lost in an enchanted world in which she was a queen, among magical palaces, with marvelous amours . . .

Thus she lived, satisfied; but she learned soon enough that reality is not the sister of dream, and her practical debut in the knowledge of things forbidden to little maidens lacked grandeur.

That occurred one evening in July in a large abandoned waste-ground full of long grass and bushes, where she had taken refuge before going home for dinner to her mother's stifling shop. A scapegrace of her own age, who had curly hair and whom she knew well, joined her by sliding, as she had done, between two dislocated planks in the fence, and having drawn near to her, in a sly and awkward manner, with no other preamble but vague sniggers, asked her if she knew what the difference was between men and women.

"Women have long hair and no beard," Gabrielle replied, with a naivety that was not exempt from dissimulation.

"That's not all," the boy replied. "The beard can be shaved, and women . . ." He stopped, in spite of his natural impudence. He blushed slightly, hesitated, and made a decision. "The difference is there," he said, with a gesture.

"Oh!" said Gabrielle, recoiling, shocked but curious, and added: "That's not true!"

"It's true," said the boy, whose ears were red and whose voice was even hoarser than usual. "Would you like me to show you? You can show me too."

"You're dirty," said Gaby. "I'm going to tell Maman."

A vain threat. She stayed, still telling herself that she was going to go. The conversation continued, punctuated by embarrassed silences and anxious shivers . . . and Gaby ended up wanting to observe the difference, and to show it, provided that no dirty words were spoken. None were, and the exchange took place . . .

Gaby lifted up her dress; two faces, reddened to the ears, looked up at the same time; embarrassed eyes met.

"You're disgusting!" Gaby exclaimed, suddenly bursting into sobs.

And she fled at a run.

Gabrielle conserved of that visual initiation a memory of shame and troubled joy. She maintained in appearance an irreducible hatred for the curly-haired scapegrace, and a grateful affection for the waste ground that had drawn her into her first adventure, inglorious as it was.

After a while, the waste ground and the abandoned gardens became forests in miniature, where little wild beasts lived freely in the midst of the profound tumult of the city. Between the bushes and the clumps of grass, under dead leaves, the brown and yellow earth was visible. Birds nested in the branches, whose leaves obstructed the view from the adjacent houses in summer. The wind howled during winter nights and the rains of spring streamed down the slopes, hollowing out torrents, which went to drown the wild rats in their holes, in the midst of the rejuvenated grass.

Gabrielle was soon familiar with all the enclosures in her neighborhood, of which there were many. She knew those in which the most tranquility, and the least troubled solitude, reigned. She introduced herself into them easily, by climbing some low fence or sliding between dislocated planks. She chose the largest, the most uncultivated and, especially, the ones least frequented by the urchins of the neighborhood.

She spent long hours there, on fine days, dreaming her childish dreams of happiness and sumptuousness. Something new was now mixed into them, and the memory of the scapegrace with the curly hair gave her ideas to complete her imaginary adventures. Mythological stories were alloyed with the novels whose deadly attractions she was beginning to savor, fabricating for her a world that was quite unreal but which gradually took on more importance for her, and which caused her increasing desolation in seeing how different the constituents of everyday life were: the shop, with its common and dirty washerwomen; the obscene jokes or sentimental stupidities of street urchins or petty employees; the libidinous pursuits of old gentlemen hunting in the streets; and even the exaggerated tenderness of her mother, who was no longer able to refuse her anything and let her do as she wished.

Gaby reached her sixteenth year thus. She had long dresses and more coquetry, and her mother spoke to her insistently about the Conservatoire. She shook her head and smiled; she wanted to be happy, but not to take any trouble over it. Then too, her dreamy little girl's mind was still the same, and she liked her liberty too much to consent to a harder school than that of the old lady with the qualifications, who had just died.

She was slightly melancholy, however, for she was very desirous of amour, but none of those surrounding her seemed worthy of her. The idea of surrendering herself to the curly-haired scapegrace, who pursued her obstinately, or to any of his peers, horrified her . . . and she wondered when the one for whom she was saving herself would come.

Gabrielle was sad that morning, and took refuge in the most profound of her waste grounds, the one that was so big that she was not sure of knowing all its turnings, and which had been abandoned for so long that the concierge on the far side of the road, who was at least eighty, said that it had always been thus, and that the dilapidated old walls, the immense wild field and the great gnarled trees had never had a master.

Gabrielle had turned into the deserted side-street, and opened the big worm-eaten door, for which she had contrived, with one of those cajoleries that always succeeded, to be entrusted with a key, for there was no means of climbing in. She closed the heavy batten with the sensual feeling of entering into solitude, and the verdant expanse was hers. The May dew was still softening the soil, but the sun, the divine archer, was launching his golden arrows between the fresh leaves and making the dewdrops suspended in the grass scintillate as Gaby rapturously moistened her shoes therein.

She followed the effaced pathways where new verdure was trembling, and eventually reached her favorite spot: an old arbor sheltered from the wind and rain by a roof and partitions of elder branches interwoven with climbing plants. In that covert there was the enervating heat of a hothouse, and the leaves filtered a green shade patched here and there with pale rays of sunlight. Aromas emerged from the earth and the trees . . .

Gabrielle felt herself invaded by a voluptuous laziness, and her thoughts drifted, delighting in the mythological dreams she had been taught. She evoked, in accordance with what she knew of them, the fabulous times when the gods and mortals had talked to one another and loved one another, in which all the things of the earth had been animated by a mysterious soul, when the sylvans, satyrs and fauns haunted the profound woods with their ambiguous forms, their amorous games, their lascivious laughing pursuits . . .

She thought that she was a nymph forgotten by time, and her dream, outside life and outside time, cradled her softly in the eternal emotion of spring, sunlight and amorous desire.

Suddenly, in the happy unconsciousness into which she had plunged, she heard the sound of a slight rustling of branches, and a head appeared between the leaves. Gaby shuddered, but did not move. The branches parted further, a face appeared, and Gaby recognized the form of her dream.

The being parted the branches with his bare shoulders and arms, and leaned forward to consider her, his face attentive and bearded. He seemed to be young. A crown of ivy around the temples mingled the short curls with dark and shiny leaves, which did not conceal the little backwardly-curved horns. He bore some resemblance to the urchin who had once shown her the difference, but Gabriele did not perceive any; she thought, without astonishment, that the adventure had finally arrived, proving the extent to which it was her that had reckoned with everyone else in the world . . .

She remained motionless. Feigning sleep, she was half-recumbent, and her dress was raised over her bent knee, allowing the other round and slender leg to be seen, molded in its bright stocking. Emption swelled her young breasts, and the slack neckline yawned slightly over the moist skin.

The faun's eyes were shining like the morning dew; desire dilated his broad nostrils. He laughed soundlessly, showing his white teeth, and advanced.

Gabrielle observed him, between half-closed eye-lashes. He seemed a trifle breathless; short hair curled on his muscular chest and the little hooves terminating his rigid and hairy legs placed themselves soundlessly in the soft grass.

He leaned over Gabrielle and gently picked up the hem of her dress, which he lifted up slightly. She could not help making a slight movement, but he stopped immediately—ready, it seemed, to flee. Then she remained motionless, and he resumed, lifting the pleats of the supple fabric. He fixed his ardent and joyful eyes on the pretty legs, which he gradually uncovered all the way to the top.

Gaby gathered all her strength in order not to budge. That gaze, lingering upon her, searching avidly, in the imperceptible gap in the cloth, for the scarcely-revealed flesh, stimulated her to the point of crying out, but she was too afraid that the apparition might vanish . . .

And she felt a small, strong, slightly tremulous hand groping around her waist to undo the buttons of her girdle, which then pulled away the light fabric under the lifted dress . . .

With the obliging desire to assist the operation, with no further thought of her modesty—had anyone had any, in mythological days?—she raised herself up slightly . . . and sensed that she was nude from the waist to the knees. The cool caress of the air made her shiver. Her corsage was undone, and her breasts, beneath a small avid hand, erected their virginal tips . . .

Another hand made her shudder profoundly in an instinctive and intimate revolt . . . but already, the warm and hairy body had descended upon her; she saw the laughing red face right up against her face, the kiss of bearded lips opened her lips and she felt a tearing pain that convulsed her fibers and made her clench her teeth in order not to scream. Then that went more smoothly, and she surrendered herself gladly to all that was demanded of her by the mythological lasciviousness of the man with goat's feet.

✳

Thus occurred the amorous initiation of Gabrielle, an imaginative and sensual little girl who had dreamed dreams that were not of her time . . .

The joys of that morning were never renewed for her. At noon, drunk with love, she quit her mysterious lover, saying to him "until tomorrow"—but it was forever. When she came back the next day, there was an army of workmen—malevolent gnomes, she thought—ravaging the great poetic terrain, demolishing the old walls and clearing the profound wild thickets. To the questions of the distressed Gabrielle they replied with jokes and lewd comments. The former owner had died and his heir wanted to have houses constructed to rent out.

Gabrielle searched fruitlessly for the being who had taken her on that May morning. She never saw him again, for the creatures of his species shun the tumult of workplaces, and their fabulous appearance cannot manifest itself in cobbled streets or the meager little gardens of modern houses.

Gabrielle was in despair, but, with time, as she was a good little girl and it was necessary to live, and to live happily in relative luxury and idleness, she became a courtesan.

She obtained a dazzling success in that art, which gave her glory and money, but never made her forget her first and fabulous lover, who remained the best.

VENUS AND THE FAUN

by Paul Adam

A S in every radiant dawn, Venus, in order to please herself, sprang from the marine waves. Her legs were still two sprays of foam at the summit of a galloping wave; playing the siren amused the goddess. She allowed the wave from which she was born to cross the extent of the gray and blue water, traveling the indefinite frissons of the peaceful element that sometimes darkened and sometimes brightened. In front of her, in the successive wrinkles of the Ocean, golden needles were raining. The goddess smiled, and her night-dark eyes gazed at the wheel of the chariot that Phoebus was driving, climbing the curved path of the sky, for she perceived the person who remained invisible to human beings, dazzled before being able to sustain his glare.

When the beach appeared, amid the scents of distant meadows and woods, Venus ceased to cherish the liquid. She thought that robust flesh seduces Eros, and her legs completed their affirmation. Radiant and white, she permitted the wave to bear her straight over the reptilian spine that overflowed gently and died down, a broad pellicle of foamy and tremulous water, quickly vanished beneath her Olympian feet.

The great rocks resounded. The sand curved inwards like a breast desirous of inhaling all of space. Venus shone like the salt of the sea, like the nacre of roseate sea-shells. Her perfumes stirred the goats that were grazing on top of the cliff. Further away, two billy-goats were pursuing one another. A third individual joined in their race. He was trotting vigorously on his two hind feet, which sank into the ground, and the goddess recognized a faun by his broad agile arms, his gray beard and his virile breast.

He grabbed each goat by one horn. He dragged them away in spite of their impetuous resistance and the malice of their sly gaze. He leapt from stone to stone with his yellow-coated captives. Muscles swelled his bronze limbs; pebbles tumbled with them down the slope, all the way to the cascades of the sea assailing the reefs . . .

Suddenly, he stopped before the goddess. "Venus, I dedicate these indefatigable males to you," he cried. "See, my strength has tamed them. If it is permitted to a modest sylvan to raise his prayers as far as you, daughter of the harmonious Fates, accept the sacrifice of one who wishes to embrace, at least in dream, your immortal appearance!"

So saying, and holding out his arms, he lifted the two caprine victims from the ground. In his motionless fists, the goats writhed, running in the air, but they were unable to move anything, neither his short hamstrings, nor his obese belly, nor his knotty and hairy torso—nothing except the mocking smile of the face creased around the pug nose.

Venus was interested in the ugliness of the supplicant.

"Tutelary," he went on, "shall I invoke you in vain? Will you not deign to gratify my sleep with an unparalleled dream? It is not because I intend to imagine, during the blissful illusion being your industrious spouse, who forges the history of States on the shields of heroes. I am not similar to Jupiter, of whom the graces were conceived in your propitious loins, even less to Bacchus, whose ardor enabled you to give birth to Priapus, a model that I emulate before hamadryads chosen as arbiter . . . far be it from me to nurture such sacrilegious ambitions. Would it be fitting for me to envy the one who is the devastating arm of the Causes, the fathers of the world? How would it serve my ignorance to know the eternal intoxication by means of which the son of Semele conceives the mysteries of the secret laws that link souls, assembles them into tribes and peoples, provides them with civilizing arts and makes bestial races serve them as he harnesses his chariot to tigers?[1]

"Have no fear that I want to cry to the four corners of the horizon the furies of Mars, who has conquered you. Rather would I wish for the fate of Mercury, who rendered you mother of Hermaphrodite, since he can admire his descendants in the doubly sexed image perpetuated by your embrace. But that I dare not desire. O face of Nature, accept, at least, these first fruits of the amorous earth, which I offer you before the foam of the wave. See, Amphitrite herself, or your mother Dionea, are making the prescribed libations here. I shall immolate the victims myself by striking their heads to-

---

1 According to some accounts, Dionysus was the son of Semele.

gether like these stones from which one provokes the movement of flame and its fecund heat, the sources of Being. O Goddess, an undulating flame of warm blood will emerge from their split skulls. Like Eros, my desire launches forward from my spirit toward your beauty, Venus Anadyomene, over which the brightness of the water streams. Accept these two goats.

"On high, Phoebus is stimulating the fire of your mother Dionea's altar, pouring the sacred flux of which you made the essential pearl in coming ashore in my domain. Be welcome on the fine gold of the sand on which I roll, on the crest of the cliff where I adore the expanse, in the cool of the grotto where I dream of you; and, if you also want it, in the melodious forest that sings by means of the ices of the birds, rustles by virtue of hidden streams, bells by virtue of rutting stags and laughs by means of the eyes of satyrs and nymphs. Lift your finger of dawn and I will accomplish the sacrifice before your majestic feet . . ."

Thus spoke the faun. Neither his thick-lipped mouth nor the gleaming orbs of his eyes moved, but his desire was evident.

"Assuredly," the goddess replied, "it is favorable to consider you in the light of day, your arms extended like a man whom the sacrificer has nailed to the crucial and sacred instrument of which the branches in turning one over the other, produce the spark for which Prometheus is suffering on the cliff of the Caucasus. But will a dream be sufficient for you? Do you not fear that the memory of your illusory emotion might haunt you eternally and constrain you to seek my charm in all women, no matter how poorly endowed with charm by Hermeros? Those whom you solicit will often escape you. Youth is tempting; you do not possess it. Noble beauty enchants; it scarcely adorns your rugged face with gross wrinkles, which the rain and heat-waves have long obliged to grimace.

"Dreams do not satisfy; they incite to veritable satiations. You do not know what you are asking, unfortunate individual. After the unreal taste of my breath, even that of zephyr would appear intolerable to you. After the unreal savor of my breasts you would reject the ripe fruits that Pomona has gathered from the garden of the Hesperus. After the unreal softness of my embrace you would no longer be able to suffer the roughness of the spring air. After the unreal shocks of our pleasures, you would judge insipid and languid the beating of your heart, even when it follows the race at the end of which you would seize the antler of the swiftest stag fleeing over the altitudes of the mountain. Only my kiss of flesh appeases.

"Render liberty, then, to those two goats exhausted by fear, which your swollen muscles are holding suspended. Your prayer is foolish. You are asking that I inflict the punishment upon you reserved by my hatred for my most redoubtable enemies. On them I lavish the dreams of which you are requesting the mortal favor. Then they die. Your semi-divine quality would not permit you that repose. Your days would flow eternally, miserable and insipid, in the inactive old age of mind and limb. No mundane attraction would content you. Faun, faun, beg me not to accept your sacrifice. Put those propitiatory animals down . . . and go and play with them among the fleeing nymphs and mischievous goats. Unless . . ."

Venus fell silent. She put her auroral finger over her crepuscular lips. The profound and stellar night of her eyes aspired the tremulous soul of her zealot. The goats fell on to their hooves and fed along a rocky path toward the crest of the cliff.

"Daughter of Ocean," cried the unhappy faun, "is it a blasphemy that you are counseling me? Are you demanding of me that I incur the atrocious penalty of a sacrilege in asking you to unite yourself with my infimal nature . . . ?"

"Finish," she said, "if you are intrepid, if you are able to see without paling the vapors of the Acheron animate the phantoms that the Eumenides enchain to the loins of blasphemers . . ."

The faun thought that his bones were cleaving in all his limbs, so terrible was the chastisement evoked by the melodious voice of Cypris. However, she had not furrowed the black eyebrows of her scintillating face. He even thought that a benevolent mockery emanated from the goddess. She was not so much a great light as a beautiful voluptuous woman ready to smile.

"O you who are adored in all the places where virgins dazzle the gazes of mortals, do you mean that you are putting my courage to the test?" he cried. "Do you mean that if I dare to confront the risk of the atrocious, eternal penalty, perhaps to obtain you, you would recompense my audacity by inclining as far as me? O Cythera, if it pleases you that I must pay with infinite tortures for the brief glory that my life desires, even that price would seem mediocre to my desire. If the blasphemy of wanting the good fortune of Anchises, who has moaned in your arms, can win me, before the vengeance of the ingenious Furies, the felicity of Anchises, are you not aware, joy of Olympus, that I am consecrating myself already, without dread, to their viperine whips, for all time. Nothing within me trembles but the dread of being mistaken as to the meaning of the smile that is born at the corners of your solar mouth . . . !"

While he was speaking, the crafty wife of Vulcan attenuated the unsustainable glare of her splendor, and her divine stature diminished, in order to adapt to that of the supplicant.

"Faun," she said, "I grant your wishes, since I have read in your intelligence the frank audacity of accepting the trade between my kiss and your mild life, prey henceforth to the deadly work of the Eumenides. The excess of your hideousness and your strength tempts me. It pleases me to sense against me and within me the intoxication of a being that surprises the least expected and most delirious felicity.

"Advance, therefore, don't be misled. It's really me, Venus. Here I am, reduced to your measure in order that you might savor my divine flesh at your ease. But I haven't changed. Just now I was as gigantic as the profound space that goes from the bosom of the sea to the chariot of Phoebus. You could not perceive it because the proportion of my limbs, my body and my heads remained such that their harmony excluded by their excellent harmony your conception of the gigantic or the minuscule. Contemplating my beauty, you admire the relationships of the parts that it assembles, whether I magnify or reduce myself to equal you in stature those relationships are not altered. I am always the same, between your sylvan arms or those of the World, the father of us all.

"Advance. In truth, I am the excellent Anadyomene, the joy of Olympus and the mother of that Priapus, the competitor that you must vanquish if you hope to turn away by some means the fatal wrath of the Eumenides. Advance . . . Venus is lying down upon the warm sand in order to receive the impetuous kiss of a faun who has temerity to the point of not dreading the most terrible of the tortures imagined by the gods and humans . . . Yes, it is my divinity that you are touching, naïve brute who flowers in the moist mud of the forest."

Thus Venus and the faun made love in the soft sand from the blood of the dawn until the blood of the dusk.

"Those two moments," said Venus, "are the victims of my sacrifice to the Universe. Our pleasure has brought them into collision one against the other, for the time that ordinarily separates them has not existed for us. The two bloods have mingled in one alone, the spark of fulgurant voluptuousness. O my lover, you are palpitating and your desire is not weary. You are surpassing the fecundity of my son Priapus himself. The Eumenides will not prevail against you . . . in accordance with my promise, since the desire of the earth has sated the creative desire of the Fates. The work of the gods is worthy of the gods, and I have discovered in you the new mirror of their genius . . ."

The faun was crouching down; malicious and mocking, he combed his beard with his fingernails. His eyelids blinked.

"Do you think so?" he said simply.

Venus laughed, then got up and shook her hair, which hid the sky and the sea in its golden turbulence.

"I want to make you a present. Choose in the city that humans will construct in my honor on the gulf, that which will always represent me to your amour. You don't know? Remember the city in fête traversed by processions and their triumphant buccinas. You visit it, however, on market days, when, disguised in your laborer's tunic, you rub up against the women packed in the multitude and splash them with lees. What do you want? My statue, which rises in the center of the temple? An illustrious sculptor fashioned it. Even I have the pleasure of recognizing myself in it, as much as that can be . . ."

"It's a false Venus," he replied. "In the temple there are also golden crowns and jewels that simulate roses and myrtles—false roses and false myrtles! I don't care about them. The countryside offers me veritable ones, which seem to me to be far more delicate. How can humans abuse themselves to the extent of recognizing in a fragment of grossly worked metal the frail and inimitable perfections of nature? I refuse your present. No effigy can resemble you, for no simulacrum of art can resemble the original of which it prides itself unduly of appearing to copy. And that is why you disdain Vulcan, the incomparable sculptor, to the joy of certain gods, a few heroes, and even a bold faun. O goddess, do you believe that I would like to see the cedar woods where I reside replaced by a forest of polished crosses garnished with gold, such as judges, priests and archons wear? What shade would those sticks give me, which goldsmiths constellate with gems and gird with metal? I have my cedars. By the same token, what would I do with a statue of Venus? I have my memory of Venus."

Then he recognized, in the extended hand of the goddess, the temple with its fronton of limpid marble, its straight columns, its precisely-marked parvis, its simple Paros marble capitals, all the harmony of its pure lines with exactly-measured proportions. Suddenly, he no longer understood whether Venus had grown to the extent of being able to hold the whole construction of the edifice in the palm of her hand, or whether the goddess was presenting him with a miniature copy of her sacred dwelling in a hand of human dimensions. He admired the fact that he could not succeed in divining it.

"Oh, Cypris," he said, "this imitates nothing but the lines invisible under the forms of nature. This only depends on the genius of humans. It only copies their subtle and calculating thought in inventing the proportions of your dwelling. In your example, no matter how large in dimension it might become nor how tiny it might shrink, the temple would retain your beauty. O daughter of the Fates, that is the very faithful effigy of your magnificence. And if you give it to me, I will receive it willingly with pious hands."

"Take it," Venus offered, "and you will no longer forget the least of the sensualities that we caused to sob together over the sand, from the blood of the dawn to the blood of the dusk."

She spoke, and she dissipated. But the faun, putting the temple to his ear like a sea-shell, was able to listen eternally to the goddess of the Hellenes smiling.

PAN'S FLUTE

by J. H. Rosny

USK was already falling. The beautiful sycamores extended enormous shadows over the river and the tall reeds. The yellow sun was seen setting and the moon rising, as pale as a silver cloud.

Lycaon savored the charming moment when the daughter and son of Latona occupied the edge of the horizon simultaneously. Covered in the dust of the roads, he was carrying a lyre of blackened wood, for he was an aede, having received the education of singers and philosophers under elegant porticoes, and the caresses of painted slaves on ivory beds, in the odor of aromatic plants, amid the harmony of musical instruments. He also remembered, both pleasantly and bitterly, industrious courtesans who knew the art of converting human sighs into gold.

And he was traveling through Hellas of the hundred cities in order to find his chimera. He sang as he went, on the agoras of cities and the edges of villages, and the kindly soil of Achaea gave him hospitality, clothing and amour in exchange. He knew how to relate the legends that please young women and how to draw the instruction therefrom that invites sensuality.

He had arrived at the Ladon of the grassy banks. In the divine half-light, he dreamed about the son of Laertes, the destroyer of ramparts, and Nausicaa with the white arms. How pleasant it would be to see her appear amid the willows of the river, with her semi-naked followers, laughing through their wet hair!

As he was thinking that, exhausted by fatigue, with his heart full of the charm of Eros, he heard silvery laughter that was prolonged amid the song of naiads. He stopped, and looked.

The red sun was about to disappear; the large moon resembled an immense mirror in which a hill was reflected. And among the slender trees, over the reeds and the lotus, he saw nymphs or mortals, scarcely clad in pure wool, who were letting their hair dry. In the crimson and white light they were as brilliant as the daughter of Antinous and her companions.

And one of them, who seemed coiffed in radiance and woven of lilies, made him think that peoples might not have been unready to suffer for her, as for Helen.

Meanwhile, he moved forward. The sparkling young women, finally perceiving him, got to their feet in order to flee across the meadows; but he raised his hands and shouted in a soft voice exercised by music and eloquence:

"Oh! Goddesses or mortals, luminous daughters of the earth, or naiads issued from the waters, have no fear of the solitary traveler. He cannot do you any harm. Rather listen to his voice . . . for I know stories of the men of old and the songs of good aedes. Would you not like me to relate for you the misfortune of Syrinx, daughter of this river of the transparent gulfs: Syrinx, who could only flee the hairy god with the goat's legs by becoming a slender reed? That story is charming on summer nights, and full of secret lessons."

The young woman who seemed to be coiffed by radiance stopped, and then the others. They all approached the aede with the gestures of curious hinds with large starlit eyes, and one of them shouted: "Tell us the story of the nymph Syrinx, stranger. We will listen to it mingle with the voice of the river. But first take a cup of dark wine, gentle on the heart."

She picked up a goatskin full of wine and poured a cupful for Lycaon. He raised the cup toward the sky, made a small libation to the river, and savored the beverage, the winged soul of which filled him with eloquence.

"Now I will tell you the story of Syrinx, issue of the river Ladon, and the terrible god who, prowling the woods and the meadows, renders the darkness more menacing."

They sat down beside him. He respired the pleasant odor of their flesh, and saw their mouths shining crimson and silver in the light of Hecate. His breast palpitated with sensuality while he tuned his sonorous lyre; the largest of the stars came to mirror themselves in the water and in the eyes of the beautiful young women, and a breath sometimes descended that seemed perfumed with the ambrosia of a god hovering in the crystalline twilight.

Lycaon first made audible the little euphonic nymphs that are captive in the strings of the lyre, and then he spoke.

✳

So, the god Pan was hiding from the gods and from men; that is why old Hesiod did not know him. He hid in the noise of tempests, in the murmur of trees, and in the sudden voices that throw panic into livestock, travelers and armies in battle. He haunted the forests that moaned, he howled with the voice of invisible wolves, the anger of equinoxes and the resonance of the sea.

Now, the nymph Syrinx lived near the river, her father, in the scintillating meadows, on the shady islands and beside tranquil coves. She was tremulous and supple, she glided happily on moonbeams; she disappeared silently into the trunks of willows; she wove her red hair with fresh herbs. There was no immortal more fearful. A leaf curved by the wind caused her to flee; she was afraid of looking at her own image, and the song of frogs in the marsh troubled her dreams.

As soon as dusk fell, she took shelter among the branches; she listened to the darkness while curling herself up. And that was not without pleasure. She knew the little sensualities of the fear that gives a voice to things and brings the stones of paths to live. She did not detest the fact that the smallest insect seemed terrible.

One morning, she heard footfalls following her over the meadow. She turned round and saw nothing. But the next day, as she lay down in the shade of a sycamore, she felt a warm breath on her neck and in her hair. One evening, when she was about to go into a grotto, an invisible obstacle stopped her for some time; she saw the vapor of breath rising.

She uttered a scream, and the obstacle disappeared.

After that, she was followed incessantly. The trees sighed as she passed by, the water uttered a soft plaint in receiving her figure, and she no longer dared to look at her naked flesh, for hidden eyes were looking at it at the same time as her. In spite of her fear of the dark, she no longer bathed except in the secrecy of night.

She understood that a god was smitten with her, and was troubled, like hinds by Autumn. Was it Phoebus, king of light, or the great Zeus, perfumed with ambrosia? She lay down on the moss of the forest or on odiferous grass. She dreamed about the blue flesh of the firmament, and the clouds, the sons of Saturn. She did not know whether she was quivering with fear or desire.

It seemed to her that she would have liked to summon Eros, but that she did not dare. The breath came down; she sensed the invisible god beside her young body, palpitating for the eternal hymen, the objective of being. Sometimes, a soft arm embraced her, with the friction of a torso. She thought that she was about to see, but she saw nothing but a furtive radiance, a fleeing animal, or the sight of a black bird in the sky.

One day, she was arranging her hair with iris flowers and little lively herbs. She was mirroring her golden head in a spring. And she was smiling, vaguely, at her flexible grace, while foliage quivered beside her and began to speak. And it said, in a voice that resembled the murmur of waves:

"It is the god Pan who loves you, nymph issued from the beautiful river Ladon. He wants to create new beings with you, who have no peers on earth. You will give birth to chimerical animals: lion-men and swan-women. You will put into the woods and the meadows figures that are not accustomed to be there. And you will be glorious among the immortals, for nothing is more beautiful than to be the mother of unknown forms."

The fearful nymph only understood what it said vaguely, but she found charm in the voice that quivered in the foliage, and she said, softly: "Has the god Pan no face, then, that he always speaks by means of the trees, the waters and echoes?"

The foliage replied: "The god Pan has many faces, for he is the king of all the beasts and all the satyrs who live among the trees . . . and who are modeled in his resemblance."

But the nymph with the bright eyes still did not understand. She said in her turn: "What is the point of so many faces, if they cannot make themselves visible?"

As she spoke, the foliage started to laugh.

"Would you like to see Pan, innocent nymph?"

She trembled, but curiosity was stronger than fear.

"Yes."

"Look!"

She saw a reflection, and then a large stag with ten branches. It threw its head back and pawed the grass with its cloven hoof. Its eyes sparkled like the red stars of Ares; ardor elevated its muscular flanks. It came toward the nymph and placed its warm mouth on her shoulder. She sensed the ardor of Eros in that agile guest of the forests, and wanted to recoil. But she found herself pressed against the vast trunk of an oak; the powerful beast caressed her white breast, and her shoulders, comparable to those of silver Hebe. Thus the wild bull on the Phoenician shore mingled its breath with that of the pale Europa.

Syrinx uttered a loud scream of fear. The stag looked at her then with its bright eyes, raised its branched horns and vanished like a cloud.

"You have seen one of the faces of the god Pan," murmured the foliage. "But he can also take on human form."

Syrinx was still shivering. The gaze of the stag was within her, like a fire in a hearth. Eternal life excited her to abandon herself, for the benefit of beings that were to be born in the future. She desired to see Pan in human form, and said so in a whisper to the foliage.

Then, in the blue shade, a human face appeared. It bore a forked beard, and horns on the head; his body was covered with unkempt hair, and his limbs were those of a goat. And his eyes were resplendent with the same red flame that had appeared in the stag's eyes.

"Syrinx, tremulous daughter of the waters and the meadows, your destiny will be as sweet as Echo, to whom I gave Iynx, and Aega, who conceived Aegipan. I am the great god of the future. My descendants will populate the earth when those of Zeus, Poseidon and Phoebus are hidden in sad dwellings and disdained by men. Come, nymph with the beautiful tresses, we shall be happy on the profound moss. We shall unite in order to make the forest more mysterious."

He spoke, but Syrinx disdained his hairy body and his horned head. She rose to her feet nimbly and tried to flee toward the river with the beautiful eddies; but the god barred her route. She raised her hands toward the heavens and prayed:

"Zeus, O Father who reigns from the heights of Ida, very great, very glorious, and you, Phoebus, conductor of light, and you, divine River who gave birth to me, have pity on me; do not let me fall into the hands of this brutal god."

"Your prayer is vain, Syrinx," said the god Pan, "for I am the master of nymphs born of rivers. It is insensate, for you are refusing happiness . . ."

"Change your face!" cried the nymph. "I cannot abide your goat's feet and your hairy torso . . ."

"It is the form in which I desire to be a father . . . there is none more beautiful."

She fled toward the hills. She bounded like a filly that has not yet known the human yoke; he followed her like a proud stallion, the king of herds. They ran over pastures, hills and plains where men live who nourish themselves on wheat. And when dusk fell, and the shadows of the trees were elongated, when they both returned toward the Ladon, whose bend they had cut across, Pan cried:

"Stop, Syrinx. Fear, in fleeing the decree of Eros, running to your doom. The River itself cannot protect you, and for having escaped destiny, you would be similar to a sterile herb."

"I would rather be similar to a reed." she replied, "than be the mother of a satyr . . ."

As she spoke, the river appeared, all red in the dusk. It appeared for a moment that Syrinx was finally about to reach it, but as she was already throwing herself into the water, Pan extended his arms and touched the fugitive nymph.

He was holding nothing but a long, flexible reed . . .

The aede stopped speaking; the young women remained silent. They were moved; their breasts were rising gently.

A violet light descended through the branches. The river scintillated among the reeds; the population of frogs sang in a melancholy fashion.

Lycaon went on: "The great god Pan cut the reed and made the amorous flute that it is so sweet to hear on fine evenings. Thus, the nymph who died for not having wanted amour took on the voice of amour, and the flute sings the eternal regret of young women who, like her, die sterile. For they are dead among the dead! It is necessary to love, virgins similar to the Immortals . . . even if the lover is animal as well as divine. He has caprine feet as well as starry eyes; his body is hairy but his action is magnificent. Those who have scorned him will never be anything but plaintive reeds . . .

"It is said," he added, "that on beautiful evenings, when the air is tranquil and rivers sleep like living beings, that those who are ripe for Eros hear the sounds of the flute rising on the shores of lakes, rivers or marshes. That is the melancholy Syrinx, who is exhorting them not to be pitiless for themselves, and to savor the felicity of being conquered."

At those words, young ears were directed toward the river. Nothing could be heard but the slight movement of the waves, the noise of the batrachians and quivering foliage, but Agamede, crowned with radiance, turned her beautiful eyes toward the aede and murmured in an emotional voice:

"I can hear the voice of Syrinx . . ."

She had allowed her veil to fall, and her youthful cleavage was visible in the moonlight. She was listening, attentively, to the faint flute whose moaning she alone could hear.

Lycaon sensed the terrible soft flame for which generations of men live and perish, and which caused the black ships of the Achaeans to depart in order to recover the daughter of Leda from the Trojan horse-tamers.

He said:

"It's the voice of the god, charming young woman. Beware of resisting him . . ."

"I have no desire to resist him," she replied.

She stood up, happy to be submissive, already letting down her long hair made of light and gold. Her companions did not murmur, for they believed that they recognized the mysterious will that no more permits the disputation of the sacrifice of a young woman than the sacrifice of a dove.

And the aede prayed:

"Be propitious to us, god of the invincible arrows, who reigns ardently over Thespis, you who conducted me to these divine shores. I shall ornament your magnificent altar, in Samos or in Crete . . . but could I offer you a victim, more superb than this one, a priestess more splendid and better made to celebrate your glorious mysteries?"

The voice and the lyre fell silent. The aede carried his ravishing prey away.

While the aede united his mouth with unknown young lips, behind the willows, in the embalmed shade, where fireflies shone like little mortal stars, the Arcadian chorus sang the light hymn of Aphrodite; and the delicious soul of Hellas, which knew how to make beauty a glory and amour a virtue, floated over the silvery waters of the river, in an atmosphere so diaphanous that it seemed that the sky and all the stars were touching the crowns of the trees.

THE MASK OF THE FAUN

by Saint-Blancard

THE fantasy of an ancestor had animated the park with a population of antique statues. Dianas, Antinous, Venuses and the whole legion of amiable gods and goddesses enlivened the mysterious arbors with the marmoreal note of their polished bodies, surprised when encountered suddenly at the center of the intersections where so many broad paths bordered by centenarian trees converged. Sometimes capricious routes bristling with brambles seemed, on the edges of ponds, to reflect the grace of their forms, allowing themselves to be caressed by the breeze charged with the voluptuous perfume of wild flowers.

Having escaped by a miracle the symmetrical raking rage of the gardeners, very close to the house, one corner of verdure had survived the affront of borders and expertly ordered bushes. It was a vast hemicycle whose vault and sides were formed by the tangled branches of trees, and whose seating had been arranged in grassy steps. In front, a broad clearing surrounded bushes growing at whim. The thickness of the leafy vault, preventing the sun from penetrating, only allowed a gently discreet light to reach it, and toward the back the dormant water of a large basin stagnated, flowery with irises, nenuphars and arums. The glaucous water in the foreground was brightened by a kind of gap in the mass of verdure, a mirror that rendered mobile the sway of the lighter trees trembling in the sunlight. The mask of a faun looming up in the form common to Hermes on a small quadrangular marble plinth imposed a white note on the velvety profundity of the foliage.

Happy to escape the gaze of her masters, to be able to read avidly, in peace, the hopefully indecent book removed from the château library, the governess charged with the education of Marthe Simier often took her to play in that place. The faun was a friend, and when comrades came to see her he was ornamented with all the flowers that they could gather, and the little girls made offerings to him, presenting him with cakes and fruits that they liked, circling around him or in front of him, dancing.

They were renewing, without suspecting it, the rites of an abolished worship, and the faun seemed to be smiling at them with a hearty laughter. They sometimes went as far as using familiarity toward him, and having hoisted themselves up as best they could, clusters of laughing little girls suspended themselves from his neck. The faun, in any case, continued laughing joyfully—but suddenly, the illumination changed and the shadows spread over the stone face, modifying the cheerful expression into a surly rictus. Then there were alarms and objurgations and the children fled, as light as butterflies.

Thus Marthe played with the faun, as with a doll, and continued that distraction until the age when childhood is put away in the cupboards of girls with the babies, the picture-books and the fake tea-sets.

She loved the six months spent outside the city, during which, save for the hours of lessons and sleep, she lived constantly in the open air. Nature attracted her; she experienced a keen pleasure in contemplating it and penetrating it. Only living in the country for the months of fine weather, she only knew it under the amiable aspects and spring and summer, and in its suavely melancholy impression of the beginning of autumn; she did not know the rude song of winter, during which she lived with her parents in Paris.

She grew up and passed through the age when the mind receives in deposit and retains without curiosity information that will only blossom later, when the body alone develops. It is a time of lethargy for the soul that, no longer satisfied by infantile distractions, does not worry yet about the problems of the heart or the anxieties of the future. It is a march on a plain, during which the soul receives in potential the seeds of sentiments and passions that will flourish later, good or bad, in a body that is developing slowly toward beauty or ugliness.

Marthe, however, did not neglect the arbor of the faun. She only said bonjour to him in passing, and plunged into the intoxicating reading of the books for the young. The smile of the faun no longer worried her.

Until the age of seventeen her life went by without any chagrin or trouble whatsoever corroding her serenity. But the time came when the woman was about to be born and affirm what she would always remain.

That spring, her soul opened to dreams, and her body quivered for the first time with involuntary frissons. Now she came into the arbor to repose, and the book she brought with her almost always remained closed. Problems that were still undefined were posed in her mind. She stretched herself out, gripped by a blissful lassitude never felt before, and remained there for hours, lying on the grassy steps . . .

Quivering insects pursued one another relentlessly, rapid flashes of light making their multicolored wings glitter, and suddenly disappeared into the calyx of some widely-blooming flower. With soft gestures the flowers leaned toward one another, and the branches of the trees appeared to be arms entwining and releasing one another, quitting one another in order to take up new embraces. A light sweat pearled on Marthe's forehead, troubled by the spectacle of those enlacements and pursuits, intoxicated by the perfume of honeysuckle.

Her conscious emotion became her secret, and, not daring to interrogate it, she gazed attentively at the face of the faun. He no longer had the expression of naïve joy that she had remarked as a child; she found that he was smiling enigmatically and greedily; his eyes were malicious, and for her, he soon personified one of those elements that she saw incessantly in pursuit of another. The legend of the cabbages darkened;[1] she paid attention to the fact that there were different kinds of people and that some of them were those insects pursuing other

____

1 One of the standard evasive answers given by French adults to children who ask where babies come from used to be that boys are born from cabbages and girls from roses.

members of their species. If the faun appeared to her as a symbol of one element, it was in his shadow that she was revealed to herself as the complementary element. And the mystery of attractions was awakened in her, sweet and desirable.

It was in the water that came as far as the pedestal that she saw her woman's face reflected alongside the ruder one of the faun. He was ugly, to be sure, but his physiognomy respired a desire that was common to her. When she quit the château in the autumn she went to thank him for the information she had received from him, not doubting that he had been the initiator for her. The leaves were beginning to fall; some, as they fell, were interrupted by his hair, clinging to the pointed ears of his face of stone. In the light filtered by the gray sky, the smile was modified again and appeared to become melancholy. She thought it good that it was thus, being tenderly languid at that moment, with all of nature.

However, Marthe remembered the laughing faun, joyful in considering the ardors that drew the beings of different sexes toward one another, and her curiosity required satisfaction. She listened to the cantilenas with which young men lulled her, understood the word amour and rebelled against the conventions that, for a young woman of her sort debased it as an advantageous bargain.

The spectacle of nature and the liberty of the beings that populated it caused her to scorn the paltry conventions of social contracts. She looked around her with intelligence, and debated between the principles learned by heart and those devoid of lies of natural life. The milieu in which she lived, and the situation of her parents, rendered her the victim of the former.

She believed the words of a young man who was introduced to her. Elegant, fortunate and fundamentally skeptical, it appeared to be him who would finally assure her of the reality of the dream, for he entered into her views and murmured the song of amour with such conviction that she abandoned her heart to him and agreed to marry him.

It was not long afterwards that she had the despair of perceiving her irreparable error. The man had lied, and his flexibility and his flattery had no other goal but the conquest of her fortune. Once that was obtained, he showed himself merely correct, and that was not enough for Marthe, even if it was sufficient for the spectators of their life. She was proclaimed to be a fortunate young woman, and she suffered frightfully, proud enough to dissimulate the distress of her heart, not encountering anyone around her who could understand her confidences and sympathize with her dolor, so implausible that she would not be excused for it.

Appearances did not permit her to escape her chagrin, and she became desolate in her solitude, crying out for nature but retained in the city by the occupations of the jealous husband, longing for a sojourn in the château.

Finally, she was able to take refuge there, and allowed herself to be courted there, seeking to encounter in a man the vibrancy of which her husband was incapable. She thought she had finally encountered the one who would respond to her aspirations. Then she accepted to find herself alone with him in the hemicycle where the indulgent face of the faun still blossomed, and knew further disenchantment in that commerce.

Desolate then, in despair at not encountering what she sought, she went to meditate and weep in the familiar retreat, and this time looked directly into the stone face, interrogated it, and recoiled in fear.

The mouth of the faun was dilated in laughter of immense mockery; she thought that it was about to proffer cruel sarcasms, and, furious, she threw it to the ground, were it shattered into a thousand pieces. The witness of her infantile games, her girlish laughter and her womanly desires died without being able to reveal to her the secret of amour.

SENTIMENTAL HESITATION

by Henri de Régnier

IT was the desire to exercise my discernment on a new object that made me want to be introduced to Madame de Morège. I had heard mention of her via several of my friends, and they talked about her so diversely that the different appreciations had piqued my curiosity. Their opinions only accorded on one point: Madame de Morège was charming. A few other facts remained equally beyond dispute; they established that Madame de Morège lived quite independently and somewhat retired, that she enjoyed a certain fortune, that her husband lived in Rome and only came to Paris rarely, that she occupied, in the Rue Franklin, an elegant entresol ornamented with old furniture and choice trinkets, among which she gladly received a few friends.

The Chevreau sale was the occasion when I met Madame de Morège. I asked her for permission to visit her at home, which she granted me. I returned there several times. After a certain number of visits I perceived that, not only was I in love with Madame de Morège but that I loved her madly. Yes, I loved her, and the sentiment that I experienced for her occupied me entirely. Nothing in the world existed for me any longer except my amour. I had never known a similar one for any other woman and I remained fearful and stupefied by such an imperious novelty.

Sometimes, as I went to Madame de Morège's home, which I did almost every day, I wondered what she might think of my assiduity, to which she lent herself with a good grace. My presence must have seemed inexplicable to her, unless she attributed it to my lack of occupation and idleness. In fact, although Madame de Morège's face, the timbre of her voice and the movements of her body caused me a profound rapture, I never succeeded in letting her understand anything of the pleasure and emotion that I felt in being with her. I was never able to address to her any of the compliments that a well brought up man owes to a pretty woman. So she might have thought me completely insensible to her grace and her beauty, because it appeared to me, for good reason, impossible for her to be able to divine the secret, too well hidden, of my amour.

By virtue of a particular singularity, which was added to that of my situation, the passionate sentiment that I nurtured for Madame for Morège did not render me distracted, stupid or irritable. Madame de Morège and I had long conversations about all sorts of subjects. I even contrived, in those conversations, to give evidence of wit, finesse and gaiety. I had nothing of the maladroit bewilderment that signals the amorous. My infirmity was different. It consisted simply of the impossibility of expressing my amour. Incapable of making Madame de

Morège understand how touched I was by the delights of her person, I was even more so of confessing the desire to savor the charm more intimately and tell her about the ardent and profound impression that she had made on my heart.

If, therefore, the most respectful and tender confession seemed to me to be an audacity beyond my strength, it goes without saying that the idea of ever manifesting, other than by the most indirect and vague remarks, the amour that I experienced, never even occurred to me—or, rather, only occurred to me sometimes as a whim, which I immediately sensed to be insensate and impracticable. Oh, I was far from my favorite theories regarding the opportunity that can sometimes be taken with women by choosing the propitious moment for those sorts of demonstrations.

And yet, Madame de Morège was not one of those haughty and distant individuals whose approach and behavior impose restraint and reserve. She was neither cold nor arrogant, but, on the contrary, all grace and mildness. Her simple and facile manners ought to have rendered the most delicate explanations easy. And yet, at the thought of revealing to her the state of my heart, I felt gripped with such apprehension that I weakened in advance.

Yes, that was where I was with Madame de Morège! Don't imagine, however, that I was resigned to my role as a mute lover. I suffered from it cruelly. My amour could not accommodate to being devoid of hope. I reproached myself for my cowardice, all the more so because I knew perfectly well that nothing within me would enable me to overcome it. My sole chance of coming to an end was some unexpected and prodigious circumstance that had no reason to occur, and which I was incapable of procuring.

On the other hand, I could not suppose that Madame de Morège would take responsibility for an initiative that nothing gave me reason to expect from her. There remained some mysterious intervention of hazard, but how could it be manifest? That question tortured and maddened me. For want of anything else, I had come to hope for it in the things that surrounded Madame de Morège. Her presence rendered them animate for me, Might there not be one that would talk to her about me? Might the sofa on which I sat next to her not throw me at her feet with all the might of its magical arms? Might the flowers on the drapes not quit their fabric in order to form a bouquet, which, from my hands, would carry to hers the confession of my torment?

In those uncertainties and chimeras, time passed. Several times, I tried to flee. All that I could do was to go one, two or three days without appearing in the Rue Franklin; on the fourth I rang her doorbell.

Madame de Morège was traveling. I was gripped by panic. Having gone, she might not come back! Her husband had doubtless summoned her to Rome. It was over! The domestic reassured me. Madame de Morège had gone to Nantes to see a work of art that an antiquarian had offered to her. She would be back the next day. I breathed again.

The next day, at the usual time, I was at Madame de Morège's house. Alas, she would no more know of my anguish of the previous day than she would know of my amour. Of what spell was I then prey, which reduced me to the inexplicable and dolorous silence that was consuming me, my heart hammering and my mouth sewn up? What was happening in me? Oh, it was not my youthful audacities that I regretted. What I desired was the humble power to express my secret thoughts to the woman I loved.

That was what I was reflecting on in the already gloomy drawing room where I was waiting for Madame de Morège. As the semi-obscurity rendered my wait more painful, I got up, pressed an electric switch and looked around. Suddenly, my attention was attracted by an unfamiliar object. Posed on the marble of a side-table was the figure of a faun in terra cotta. Undoubtedly, it was what had provoked Madame de Morège's journey to Nantes, and she had just brought it back from the antiquarian's home. Curiously, I examined the newcomer.

The little god was dancing. His body, modeled in sanguine earth, was capering, cheerful and brutal, elegant although rather thickset in his muscular strength. His snub-nosed, wide-mouthed face with oblique eyes and pointed ears was laughing cynically. Ardent and lively, he was dancing, holding up a bunch of grapes in his fist. One of the hooves of his two hairy legs was stamping, while the other was raising its cleft horn in a high kick.

Oh, the rude and joyful little god, rustic and sensual! The blood that reddened his limbs must only carry simple, warm and abrupt thoughts to his head. How his lips were made for kissing and his arms for hugging!

How his legs must carry him to wherever his pleasure summoned him! Oh, if only he could communicate to me a little of his strength and ardor! And I inclined before him as if to implore him.

Suddenly, the sound of the door opening made me start so abruptly that I bumped my forehead on the raised hoof of the aegipan. The shock was so unexpected that I leaned on the table and remained stunned momentarily. A sudden warmth ran through my entire body, and at the same time a surge of blood turned my face crimson. My ears were buzzing. Behind me, I thought I heard the panting breath of the Faun, whose hooves were striking the marble as if to gather for a leap. My vision was blurred.

Madame de Morège had closed the door again. She advanced toward me. I saw her smiling and mild face, while through her dress, which had become miraculously transparent, it also seemed to me that I could see her body, her supple, charming, naked body, which was coming toward me, and for which I now had bold arms and audacious hands . . .

"Confess, Paul," Madame de Morège sometimes says to me, showing me the terra cotta Faun, "confess that it was him who pushed you by the shoulders and who turned out the light."

And we look, laughing, at the little Sylvan, hilarious and drunken, whose mysterious intervention had united our ardent and silent lips in the darkness.

THE PUNISHED OUTRAGE

by Gaston Derys

IN a sinuous pathway of the Bois that leads to the lake there are a nymph and faun in white marble, who gaze at one another slyly.

Is it really in the Bois that that nymph and that faun perpetuate the splendors of pagan mysteries? I dare not affirm it categorically. The boscage of the Luxembourg and the majestic trees of the Tuileries might perhaps extend their shadow over those divine foreheads. At any rate, I have seen that nymph and that faun somewhere, in the course of a walk, and I think it was in the Bois.

In winter, statues get bored, especially mythological statues. Their nostalgia sees abolished Olympus again, and ever-clear springs, and the ever-azure sky and ever-green woods of Hellas or Sicily.

It is a common error to suppose that statues do not remember and that no thought ever palpitates beneath their temples. An occult scientist explained to me one day that statues really live—at least, those that genius has animated; for all the occult scientists in the world will never make us admit that the little plaster horrors that whiny little Italians hawk at crossroads possess a soul.

But the being who, under the chisel of a pure artist, gradually emerges from a formless block of Carrara marble, like Aphrodite from the bosom of the waves, truly exists, and mingles with universal life. If he is a god, Apollo, for instance, a little of the soul of Apollo circulates within him—only a little, for there are so many Apollos on earth. If he is a simple little faun, he might very well have the whole soul of a faun quivering within him.

"That is so true," the occult scientist also told me, "that statues are not immobile. They can move like you and me, they can talk, they can laugh and they can caress one another. But," he added with a sardonic smile, "they only deliver themselves to such frolics when there is no one around, and preferably by night. That's why people, even intelligent people, don't want to subscribe to that opinion. Folly! We don't see the earth turn, and yet it turns . . ."

Well, an adventure happened to me that corroborates the affirmations of that scientist singularly. This is it:

I dreamed, a few days ago, that I was in the Bois at midnight, in the path where the faun and the nymph gaze at one another slyly. A magnificent moonlight was pouring an extranatural light over things, and the trees were shivering in delicate opal mist. The lake, entirely frozen, was as resplendent as a silver mirror, and an impressive silence floated over the landscape.

Suddenly, a little shrill laugh troubled that silence. I turned my head and I saw the faun leap from his pedestal. He ran toward the nymph, rapid on his caprine feet, took her in his arms and deposited her on the ground.

Petrified, changed into a statue myself, I wanted to cry out, but no sound emerged from my throat. Enchained by an invincible force, it seemed to me that I was attached to the tree against which I was leaning.

After having given one another a few kisses, the faun and the nymph, holding hands, launched themselves toward the ice and executed the most graceful capers. One might have thought that they were flying, so light were they. Certainly, their feet cannot have touched the ice, and one would have sworn that they were skimming the surface of a dormant lake without troubling it.

White and harmonious, their image was reflected under their feet as in a looking-glass.

Finally, they returned to the shore.

"It's good to run," said the nymph. "Alas, through the embalmed valleys of Mytilene I ran all day like a mad thing, with my companions. And we slaked our thirst in the fresh crystal of springs. We reddened our lips and fingernails with the blood of mulberries and we chewed eglantines, which perfumed the mouth and rendered us amorous."

"And I," said the sylvan, sighing, "lay in ambush under the Ionian oaks, and I pursued the beautiful girls who passed by. In a few bounds I had quickly overtaken them, and they let themselves slide into the tender grass, invoking Diana and repeating the name of their mother. Often, they dissolved in tears, trembling like a hind forced by a hunter; but I can't remember a single one who repented of not having resisted me."

"I remember," she said, "a young shepherd whose name was Lycidas, who was as handsome as Adonis and whose kisses bruised me delectably. The day when I no longer loved him he drowned himself in the spring on the bank of which we were accustomed to meet."

"And I," cried the faun, sitting on the ground and taking his friend in his arms in order to cradle her, "still rediscover on my lips the odor of cherished lips, but my exile is mild, since you share it. And the most perfect beauties are eclipsed before yours. I perceived Cypris one day. She was walking in an olive grove with a herdsman whom she had distinguished, a large man with muscular arms, a pitiful torso and thick lips. Doves were flying around them, and roses were born under their feet. I do not say that Cypris was more desirable than you, for I cannot offend the gods, but after Cypris, you are the most beautiful woman on earth."

The nymph surrounded the goat-foot's neck with her arms, kissed him for a long time, and they delivered themselves to a pantomime the repetition of which made me conceive a high opinion of the gallant virtues of demigods.

Suddenly, a noise of footsteps was heard, and I saw three silhouettes designed in the distance

The faun pricked his little pointed ears, and I heard these rapid words distinctly:

"May the waters of the Styx swallow those wretches instantly! O nymph, it's necessary for us to resume our pedestals. Let's let them pass."

But the amorous nymph did not loosen the adorable necklace that her arms put around the shoulders of the son of Pan, and by means of halting words allowed him to understand that the moment was ill-chosen to interrupt their intercourse.

Without granting her urgent prayers, however, the faun posed his friend on her plinth and climbed slowly on to his own.

He was just in time; scarcely had he resumed his sentry duty than three men emerged before his statue. Their criminal appearance indicated that they were marauders who lie in wait by night in the Bois for belated carriages. They offered the bestial physiognomies that one encounters on the threshold of suburban taverns: low brows, evasive eyes, grimacing smiles and protruding jaws.

They stopped in front of the faun, and addressed a few sarcasms in dubious taste to him. One remarked that he must be cold; another mocked his horns; the third was greatly astonished that he had hairy legs and hooves instead of feet.

Then, for a game, the prowlers started throwing little stones at him. At that moment, I distinctly saw the nymph quiver, and her eyes appeared to me to flash.

One of the comrades tugged the faun's beard; another landed a few blows of his stick on his shoulders; they both tried to throw him to the ground.

The nymph—I can still see her gesture—extended an angry fist toward them.

Finally, after having subjected the unfortunate aegipan to all manner of teasing, one of the thieves proposed to subject him to a mutilation that has rendered the lover of Héloïse more famous than his philosophical controversies.

Coarse, ignoble laugher welcomed the suggestion of that sacrilegious project favorably.

But without leaving them time to perpetrate the outrage, the nymph bounded toward the blackguards, and launched a few punches of her marble fists at them. Howls responded. One of them fell on the gravel; the other two fled, moaning.

It was then that I woke up. It was broad daylight. Letters and newspapers were piled on a tray next to my bed. While waiting for my chocolate to be brought, I scanned the papers, and imagine my amazement on reading this item in the latest news section:

> *At about one o'clock in the morning last night, guards making their round in the Bois de Boulogne found near the lake the cadaver of a poorly dressed individual who appeared to have been struck with a sheep-bone.*

THE LAST FAUN

by Maurice Magre

I

LIGHT-FOOT had seen all his companions, the fauns with hairy human faces and goat's feet, die. Now he wandered, solitary, in deserted forests only troubled by the cries of birds and the rustle of branches.

How the earth has changed, he thought. *In the distance, I can see a boat on a pond. A bridge has been put over the torrent and over there, behind an ox, a man is marching, pushing before him a piece of iron that he is plunging into the earth. A curse upon that execrable, paltry and degenerate race, to whom the earth belongs henceforth!*

In order to shelter from the wind, Light-Foot had the custom of sleeping in a deep cavern in the mountains. It was an almost inaccessible place, in the midst of rocks.

That cavern had once served as the lair of a band of thieves, and incalculable riches were accumulated there. There were magnificent garments, jewels of every sort and barrels full of gold. Light-Foot amused himself in the evenings running the coins through his fingers. He spread them over his body or threw them into the nearby stream, unaware that humans lived and died for them.

Once, however, when he had descended the mountain and arrived near a road, he saw a man who was holding an ox by means of a rope, and who was exchanging the ox with another man for a few pieces of shiny metal. The faun went back up the mountain thoughtfully.

Since an ox, an animal astonishing in its form and weight, is given in exchange for a few pieces, I, who have a cavern full of pieces, could have a great number of oxen, and perhaps also houses and all sorts of strange objects that humans possess.

One day, the hazard of his wandering brought him to the edge of a park. He looked through a breach in the wall. At the end of the park, the form of a château was visible through the foliage. A young woman was walking along a path, a book in her hand. From time to time she stopped to read, and smiled.

But why is she smiling? he wondered.

He wanted to know the reason, and went back up to his cavern. There were a great many books here, once taken from passing merchants. They served the faun as a pillow when he slept. He looked at them at length.

That's curious; no risible thought occurs to me. Perhaps there's a secret to penetrating the meaning of these little black signs.

He went back every evening to the edge of the park, to the place where there was a breach in the wall, in order to see the young woman again.

She passed very close to him, her book in her hand, and Light-Foot's heart leapt in his breast.

Climbing trees, running through forests and scaling rocks seemed devoid of attractions to him henceforth. He wondered how he had been able to live for such a long time with such mediocre pleasures. He had attached all his happiness from now on to the breach in the wall that the young woman went past.

One evening, he made up his mind. He put his most amiable smile on his faun face; with one bound he leapt into the pathway where the young woman was walking and opened his mouth to speak.

She uttered a terrible scream and fled.

Alas, thought Light-Foot, returning to the rocks that were his domain, *I belong to a fallen race. Hair covers my face; my feet are like a goat's; I'm stooped, for I often walk on my hands as well as my feet. What a shame that my heart is possessed by the white young woman who passes through the narrow pathways of the park out there. I'll never be anything to her but an object of horror.*

Light-Foot was in despair for several days. Being simple by nature, he uttered cries and beat his breast, or ran over the rocks like an insensate for hours on end.

Finally, exhausted by fatigue, he arrived at the edge of a pool; the water was tranquil and reflected his image. He looked at it for a long time, and he thought:

In sum, I'm not so different from humans. My grandfather affirmed that humans and fauns belong to the same family. Who knows? If garments covered my body and I hid the hooves of my feet and the horns on my head, and if I studied my gait carefully, perhaps I could be mistaken for a man.

His resolution was made, for fauns act as soon as they have thought.

He cut an enormous staff in the forest and descended to the valley. A road went along it. He lay in ambush behind a tree-trunk and waited. A merchant passed by. He was an old man with a white beard. The faun ran forward and broke his head with a blow of his staff.

Fauns are unaware of the price of human life. Light-Foot loaded the merchant's body on to his back and went back up to his cavern. Then he stripped him of his garments and dressed himself in them. He plucked out the hairs covering his face as best he could; he put the merchant's large hat on his head, because two little horns emerged near his ears; he enclosed his hooves carefully in the shoes, and then he took a bag full of gold, loaded it on his back, and, thus transformed, went down the mountain and took the path that led to the nearest village.

II

Light-Foot had a palace and a carriage with lackeys in livery. He learned to read and write, and he thought. He became famous throughout the region because of his wealth and his strange appearance.

"He's a rich and worthy lord," people said of him, "who has difficulty walking, as if he were embarrassed by his shoes. He never takes his hat off for anything in the world, even when a funeral goes past. He always wears gloves, which he's never seen to take off, and high collars that hide a part of his face."

As he made generous gifts, he was well known and well liked. He called himself the Marquis of Lightfoot, and all the peasants saluted him respectfully when he passed by.

However, Light-Foot's heart was transformed. A thousand new ideas came to him because of the books he read, and he was afflicted by a strange mental illness.

He suffered cruelly—a suffering unknown to him until then—every time he thought about the white-bearded merchant he had killed with a blow of his staff. *He seemed mild and good*, he said to himself, *and I've taken away his life.*

One evening, he could not stand it any longer. He took off his shoes and his garments and he went back up to the sheer places where he had lived before, all the way to the place where he had left the merchant's body. Nothing any longer remained of it but bones bleached by the rain. Light-Foot dug a hole in the ground and put the bones in it. Then he went down again, feeling melancholy, and returned to his palace.

He thought incessantly about the young woman he had seen in the park and whom he still loved with the same amour.

One day, he said to himself: *Now I have fine clothes and I've learned the art of language, I can introduce myself to her without shame, and—who knows?—ask for her in marriage.*

So he went to the château where she lived.

He was received magnificently by the young woman's father. The latter, who was almost ruined, said to himself on seeing him: *What luck to be visited by the Marquis of Lightfoot. He's very rich; I could borrow money from him and perhaps, one day, give him my daughter in marriage.*

There was a numerous company in the drawing room; everyone surrounded Light-Foot and everyone flattered him because of his wealth. However, he had kept a hat on his head in order not to show his horns. Everyone was secretly astonished by such impoliteness, and our hero suffered a great deal from sensing that.

He came back some time after that, and the young woman's father borrowed considerable sums of money from him. But money was of no importance to Light-Foot. Beggars could knock on his door at any time; they received abundant alms. Light-Foot even lent money to rich men who had no need of money, but who asked him for it in order to profit from such uncommon generosity.

He therefore got to know the young woman he loved. He did not talk to her about love, because he did not know the manner of conversing with women on such a subject, but he questioned her father and the latter declared to him that he would be very happy to give him his daughter in marriage.

Thus, the dream of his life was about to be realized.

They were engaged one day and exchanged golden rings.

Even on that day, the Marquis of Lightfoot did not take off his glove, and the surprise was extreme.

However, Light-Foot was very unhappy.

What would my fiancée say if she knew that I was a faun? he thought.

One evening, when he was walking with her in the depths of the park, the young woman showed him the breach in the wall and said to him: "One day, I saw a frightful being bounding toward me. He was frightful to see, half man and half beast. I can't walk on this path without being afraid."

"What did he look like?" asked Light-Foot, in a tremulous voice.

"Hair covered his face. He looked like a faun."

"There are fauns whose heart is good and who are capable of love," said Light-Foot, mildly.

"It doesn't matter. I'd rather die than be touched on the tip of my finger by such a monster."

Light-Foot had heard enough. He fled. His heart was breaking in his breast. He ran at random; he lost consciousness of things. He threw away his hat, tore off his collar, which was choking him, and kicked off his shoes, which were impeding his march.

"A faun! A faun!" people cried as he passed by. And they all armed themselves with pitchforks and staffs, and launched themselves in his pursuit.

"The Marquis of Lightfoot is a faun!" That news spread like a gunpowder fuse; there was an indescribable tumult in the town.

All the people that Light-Foot had heaped with benefits, who had shared his gold, and who had eaten at his table, were now pursuing him like an animal.

Light-Foot ran straight ahead. He had emerged from the town; he had traversed fields and woods; he went up toward his birthplace.

When he was very high, among the sheer rocks, and he could no longer hear the cries of the men who were pursuing him, he cried:

"A curse on you, execrable race from which one learns dolor, proud race that will not permit a beast to raise himself as high as you! Life is devoid of charm for me henceforth. The horn of my hooves attaches me to the wild earth of the mountain, but my amorous heart summons me toward humankind!"

No one ever heard any more mention of the faun Light-Foot. But sometimes, in the evening, the young woman, wandering in the park, heard from the direction of the wall, where there was a breach, a moan so dolorous that she could not help weeping.

PAN AND THE SYRINX;
or
THE INVENTION OF THE FLUTE WITH SEVEN PIPES

by Jules Laforgue

ON his matinal three-hole pipe Pan is lamenting, letting out his very personal plaints, to the echoes of the Valley of the Variegated Grass in Arcadia. Everyone has passed through a marvelously lively valley on a beautiful summer morning, so everyone can say: "I know what that's like."

To the fortunately virginal expanse the cataracts of spring sunlight, in radiant mists of happiness and a foamy deluge of Champagne infused by the Sun itself, sprinkle the woods, the hillsides and the whole valley. O billions of prisms of optimism! O youth, O beauty, O unanimity! O sunlight!

Immortal and young, Pan has never loved as he and I understand it.

All night long, in the valley inundated by a memorable lunar solo, he has lamented bitterly on his imperfect and monotonous three-holed pipe, on his two-sou pipe. Then he ended up going to sleep. His dreams were

even emptier than his heart. At dawn he stretched himself and loosened his goat's legs, the hair on which was
fringed with dew—he no longer does gymnastics—and
now he is there, in the thyme. Face down and leaning
on his elbow, and he had recommenced the birdsong of
his distress on his three-holed pipe, which only has four
notes, and he is alone in the fine early morning solitude.
What can one do, when one *loves*, except wait like that,
in the open air, trying to express oneself through art?

Pan waits and sings thus:

> *The Other sex! The Other sex!*
> *Oh, all the little Eve*
> *Who advances, delighted by her role*
> *With her eyes illuminated*
> *By marriage,*
> *And all her hair over her shoulders*
> *In the holy light of the rising sun!*
>
> *O speak, speak!*
> *Little Eve descending from the summits,*
> *With her victim flesh*
> *And her soul all in sudden blushes!*
>
> *A body, a soul.*
> *Childhood friends!*
> *All my wife*
> *By Birth!*
>
> *And bringing vividly*
> *With her swollen heart*

The pink honey of her gums
And her breasts as timorous as leverets!

The breezes teased
The cherries of her earlobes,
And she, lifting her little nose,
Crying to the sun: "Hey, marvel!"

Then proclaiming, proudly posed:
"I'm not a little peacock,
"I'm not a doll!
"I've escaped entirely
"To come and collapse on the breast of Great Pan!
"Oh, I'm as pure as a tulip
"And virgin of principles of every sort!
"April! April!
"My happiness is hanging by a thread!"

When the fauna and the flora
Trace our duties for us
From dusk to dawn,
And from dawn to dusk!

In dreams I have seen
The little welcome Eve!
Epiphany! Epiphany!
But it's only my genius.

Pan pauses, and resumes considering the fortunately virginal morning throughout the valley—and it is the radiant morning, and all the sunlight and the universal happiness, so ungraspable! And there it is; it is up to him to make arrangements to be happy, as that morning has made arrangements to be happy.

That is easy to say. Pan abandons himself again to his imperfect but faithful pipe, worthy to be called "my old pipe." He commences the ancient ballad: *I've lost my appetite for strawberries*, and immediately stops, having lost his appetite for the ballad.

At last! The thyme quivers between his limbs, the wasps buzz, the stems of umbels are quite at ease in the charming air, the cicadas are beginning to bake with little squeals, there is happiness as far as the eye can see!

And Pan, sensing that he too has his reason for being, resumes his ritornelle of grand amour more humanly:

> *My body is ill in its beautiful soul,*
> *My beautiful soul is ill in its body,*
> *For night after night now I've called,*
> *But I still see nothing coming.*

> *It's not her flesh that will be everything to me*
> *And I'll be nothing but Great Pan for her*
> *But so what? Go play the fool*
> *In fraternal stories!*

Then he reasons aloud, in a little aside:

"O woman, woman, you who make humanity monomaniac, I love you, I love you! But what is that phrase: *Je t'aime?* Where does it come from and how does it sound, with its two inconsequential and neutral syllables. For myself, this is what I've found. *Aime* only tells me something when I associate it with that sound, and by virtue of a non-fantastic inspiration, the sound of the English word *aim*, which means *goal*. Oh, goal, yes! 'I love you' this signifies 'I tend toward you; you are my goal.' Good, just like that, I have it! That's great!"

> *Oh, will you come soon?*
> *Where can I find you,*
> *My fragile Psyche,*
> *Whom every moment deflowers*
> *For from my prosperous arms?*
>
> *Oh, it would be so you!*
> *Ingeniously I would take you*
> *Into the utmost depths of the woods,*
> *Where it is coolest;*
> *And then lay you down on the grass,*
> *After so many virginal afternoons,*
> *And abandon you to the spring*
> *In the deadening hum of cicadas*
>
> *You'll see, you'll see.*
> *That I'm not ingrate,*
> *And my arms are prosperous*
> *Like all the earth,*
> *And it's not your flesh that . . .*

"Shh! Oh, but here she is, laughing and pale, coming through the long grass of my meadow! Let's play and sing, very absorbed, in order not to alarm her. My God, My God, let her come closer then!

I've lost my appetite for strawberries,
Since I've seen in dreams
My little Eve
Smiling at me but putting
A finger over her lips.

I can say that I've lost my appetite for any mystery,
Since malign little Eve,
While smiling at me seductively,
Has made me a sign
That it's necessary to shut up!

Mystery and smile,
O my beautiful ship!

To smile and then shut up,
Oh, be silent my lute!

And it's not her flesh that will be everything to me, I swear . . .

In the early morning, in the holy sunlight, through the fortunate meadow, in fact, it is the nymph Syrinx who has advanced, unexpectedly, utterly alive, in flesh and bone—with what youth her large eyes swear it!—and who has stopped there, her gaze delighted, her neck tilted, her arms dangling, charmed by Pan's inoffensive lament, and who, believe me, in order to listen better, has gradually relaxed in the lovely thyme, albeit some distance away, but irreproachable at a distance.

Oh, it's perfectly her, rosy and modest, as marvelous as a flowering almond tree, in the meantime!

She has no shame, and knows what she is worth, in addition to all the displays that please you. But with her abundant hair put up in a very personal diadem, her large eyes brought up in elevation and her little pout, scarcely pink, she does not appear to sense that she is in the world in order to abandon herself like this to the spring, in the daze of the cicadas.

And yet, in spite of her large eyes brought up in elevation and her hair in a diadem and her distinguished pout, she was born to come here, equipped to come here.

"Yes," Pan says to himself.

"Alas," says Pan to himself, "tomorrow, and the days after tomorrow, she will have superhuman eyes no less large, and united, and her pout *of the other world.*"

But what does it matter? Pan, in his meditations, has bumped into more than one antinomy just as irreducible. And today, sick with grand amour as he is, he will accept the Woman without any argument.

He has ceased to play his little machine. He looks at her. He dare not speak yet, for fear of breaking the charm of the apparition, unmerited, after all. Let him convince himself first and penetrate himself with the idea that she is there, and that it is the present!

They look at one another: he, his teeth clenched; she, with her great eyes all one and her mouth of a small child on high, perfectly filled with being, such as she is, and devoid of highs or lows.

So, she is the one who takes it upon herself to break the charm, since there is a charm. Her voice is certainly drawling and nostalgic, but unshakably fresh.

"It's very pretty, what you were playing there."

"Oh a two-sou pipe. If only I had a more complex flute! I could do things with it! I'd no longer have any doubts."

She is silent, only asking to be interested, to be distracted in the fine weather.

"I'd no longer have any doubts," Pan insists. "Not even about . . ."

"About what?"

"About enabling you to share my old amour."

"Truly?"

She has said "truly" in an unworldly but elevated manner. And without lowering her eyes, she started smoothing the straight pleats of her short tunic, her short white tunic, lightly tightened at the waist beneath two young breasts, and fastened by a clasp at the shoulder.

"Truly?"

"Yes, but I know that it's not worth the trouble of trying, with your large eyes and that pout, charming nevertheless. No. And then, this morning I have a headache. But thank you for coming. Your presence here is very restful for me."

She is silent, her eyes all one; the weather is so beautiful!

Pan lowers his head, amusing himself shredding florets, and also blades of grass.

He raises his eyes. She is still there, at ease in the thyme, still considering him with her virginally intelligent gaze and her virginally intelligent pout.

No! One doesn't gaze with that inimitable innocence!

"When will you have finished?"

"What?"

My word! She has said "What?" with such a perfect redoubling of her eyes and her pout that Pan writhes, the Pan utters a sob in the radiant matinal solitude, a long and unique sob of amour, quite simply of amour, Pan-style.

But she must know where that sob comes from and where it is going, since she misses nothing of its tuneful perfection.

Pan, who sees that she is already frightened and holds back an "Oh, don't be afraid" that would only have made the situation worse, contents himself with saying:

"I'm ill, so ill! Oh, I understand you well! You're going to object to me, revolted, that you're passing by, that you're only an occasion. How do you know? And first of all, how do you come to be passing by here? You're not saying anything . . . Me, I'm not ingrate . . . ! Oh, well, let's leave it there."

He lowers his head and resumes shredding blades of grass and florets, like a vile maniac. He raises his eyes; she is looking at him with all her beauty, which seems decidedly pointless. What if he were to throw himself immortally at her feet in order to stun her? But he contains himself. What must come will come; everything is in Everything. And he picks up his pipe again, his old pipe, with the air of a young man for whom art is sufficient, for whom a few scales a day are sufficient.

He coos chimerically:

Beautiful eyes illuminated
By marriage!
Soul all in true sudden blushes
Flesh anointed with false trails!
It's not her flesh that would be everything to me
And I would only be the Great Pan for her,
But so what! Do what fools do
In fraternal stories!

April! April! (A dying *ritardendo* at this point.)
Our happiness is hanging by a thread!

Epiphany! Epiphany!
And then, all my genius!

Having labored sufficiently for this morning, Pan raises his head again. She is there, smiling, as if disarmed by that big baby, and also, a little, thanks to the exceptional beauty of the morning.

Pan would only have to respond to that smile with a brave smile! He thinks it more appropriate to shrug his shoulders in a superior fashion and adopt an expert expression.

"My word, what astonishing eyes you have! And that face, so thin at the base. And the pout, so legitimate! Have you sometimes dreamed of being different when you look at yourself in the mirror of a spring?"

"No, since one has the face of one's soul, so my soul couldn't imagine being more itself than my face. It's a vicious circle, I recognize that."

"It's fortunate that you're a goddess; otherwise a time would come—that of old age—when your soul would imagine a face other than yours."

"I haven't thought of that. You're quite a realist."

"I'm Pan."

"Pan who?"

"I'm . . . very little at the moment, but in general I'm everything. Understand me, it's me who is the plaint of the wind . . ."

"Aeolus, then?"

"No, understand me! I'm things, life, things, classically. No, I'm nothing. Oh, I'm very unhappy! If, at least, I had an instrument richer than this two-sou pipe! I could sing you everything that I am! Oh, I'd sing fantastically! Classical sobriety makes me laugh! *Kyries* and *Glorias in excelsis*, and the gracious and somewhat lively tunes of my homeland."

"See, men can never be clear before women. They ought to make their declaration in good French—which is to say, in noble and light Ionic dialect. No, they need music right away, the music so commonly infinite!"

Pan stood up, furious.

"And what about you women? Nothing but the sound of your own voice! You, now, solely the music of your own voice. Is that honest? Oh, poverty! Poverty on both sides, in truth!"

He falls before her in the thyme, like a dirty Caliban, and groans. She considers him with her large eyes, which are compassionate, compassionate with distinction.

Pan pulls himself together, and in a supreme tone, says: "Anyway! Look, O noble virgin, O you who you are, you who nevertheless have a familiar form; the day is advancing and I've never loved. Would you like to leave everything for me, in the name of Everything?"

A silence—wasted time, during which the entire countryside continues to be happy.

The nymph Syrinx raises herself up slowly in all her beauty. Soberly, she says: "I am the nymph Syrinx, something of a naiad too, for my father is the river Ladon, with the beautiful torso and the florid beard. I'm returning from Mount Lycabettus."

"Aha! A naiad, I see! You must find me very ugly, very Caliban, very capricant! A naiad! A cousin of the handsome Narcissus, son of the river Cephyse! Damn! He has hands, eh, Narcissus? And distinguished!"

The nymph Syrinx stiffened, moved aside a curl from her large forehead, and proclaimed in a proud and brisk voice: "You misunderstand me. I'm an esthetic soul dipped seven times in the icy water of the Castalian spring dear to the chaste Muses; I'm the most faithful of the companions of Diana . . ."

Pan recoils. Syrinx raises her arms toward the pure firmament, where Hecate is resplendent this evening; by virtue of her gesture, her two pale breasts, pure and lunar under the diaphanous tunic, rise up and are effaced proportionately.

"O Diana, Empress of pure nights, the mucus of your heart is as rough as the tongues of your mastiffs. You leap ditches and say very little. The steel of your gaze stops the rosy blood of young women who would like to go to bed immediately. The folds of your chlamys are of a purely Doric order. When one returns from your great hunts one falls like an inert mass on the dry leaves and sleeps dreamlessly until the fanfares of the dawn. To the hunt! To the hunt!"

Syrinx utters a strident burst of Valkyrie laughter and, forgetting Pan, now she starts running—oh, a young, bounding run—across the meadow and the valley, in the beautiful morning.

And Pan, his heart broken by a vast primitive sadness, watches her draw away, never to return. He stays there, suddenly depressed and very miserable, at the revelation of the state of poverty and corruption in which one decidedly lives. How pure she is thus, bounding and gazing straight ahead of her! Poor Pan. Oh, he has just had pass through his heart, like a flash of lightning, the revelation of the great and legendary dolor of Ceres, traveling the world, dusty and mendicant, interrogating shepherds, searching for her daughter Proserpine, who disappeared one morning when she was making a bouquet of wild flowers for her mother.

Amour! Amour! Do you want me to dry up on the spot, without a word, without a verse?

But Pan is immortal! And at the thought of this evening, alone with the sadness of his genius—oh, at the idea of his genius, the idea of sublime discussions in which he would charm Diana himself—Pan inhales the great air that is everyone's, and launches himself in pursuit of the precious fugitive. To the hunt! To the hunt!

And the legendary pursuit of the nymph Syrinx by the god Pan in Arcadia commences. Oh, what an adventure!

Oh, he will have her! He will put her on her knees in a corner of a wood, he will tell her what will happen, he will lower her to become his equal, and then he will be able to adore her with all his great misunderstood heart!

She is already far away. She turns round and sees that she is pursued. She stops momentarily and faces him, and then resumes her gallop, hectically.

"Oh, you're fleeing, you're fleeing! Oh, I'll have you! I'll twist your wrists, I'll crush your little kitten bones, I'll teach you!"

O long legendary day, you are far away, you will never return! This happened in Arcadia, before the advent of the Pelasgians.

The sun is everywhere, the meadows are transporting, the birds are chirping in the landscape, let the bushes take note! Couples of deer draw away from drinking, lizards stop browsing, perched on sheer rocks, and at the edge of the woods one skirts, the light bounds of the squirrels in the dry foliage break the great silence.

Oh, when he has vanquished and mastered her, that little superhuman savage, they will come to wander here, he will give her inappropriately the color of a leaf, he will never avenge himself sufficiently!

In the meantime to the hunt, to the hunt! All morning . . .

Syrinx will maintain her lead for a long time. She is not exhausted by insomnias and fevers, she has not lost the habit of gymnastics, she has slept well and lives with principle. And again, so long as they are in the plain, that continues; but when they go along the edge of a wood, Syrinx amuses herself from time to time by disappearing into the trees of the margin and Pan has to stop in order to see whether there is a trap, whether she is not going to cut through the woods and abandon the high road.

"Oh, I'll have you, I'll have you! But I'll sulk for three days and three nights. But how I love you, how I love you, how you are my goal! How beautiful your flight is! And how my Caliban heart lights up at every moment of your flight, and what beautiful tears of mine that will be worth to you this evening, once I've forgiven you!"

After the woods and the meadows and the landscapes, Syrinx finds herself confronted by a high bank that is steep and palisaded by flowering brambles. Syrinx veers obliquely and goes to climb the obstacle to one side, by means of a gentle slope, and then comes back to stand at the top, within sight of Pan, who is running dead straight. She watches him coming. And Pan, instead of going sideways like her, comes to run into the foot of that fissured wall. He stops. There is an armistice during which he goes to contemplate her thus—oh, let him at last be penetrated by that present reality! They are doubtless going to resume their discussion, which might perhaps terminate amiably, in the midday sun.

How she dominates him, irresistibly, from up there, in that noble pose, still quivering! And all her chaste and youthful person, and her hair in a solid diadem, and her large eyes all united, as virgin of insomnias as spring water is of the essence of dew! How pure and perfect her legs are, up there!

"Why are you pursuing me?" she shouts to him, in a voice habituated to launch and retain Diana's hounds.

"Because I love you! You re my goal!" he replies in his most pantheistic voice.

In his most pantheistic voice! But Syrinx, companion of Diana, is intelligent; she must have her own ideas about reproduction.

"Do you take me for an animal, a little classified animal? Don't you know that I'm inestimable?"

"And I'm an artist, someone astonishing! But fundamentally, my soul is that of a great pastor, you'll see."

"Know that my pride in remaining myself at least equals my miraculous beauty. Although I sometimes know, being a child . . ."

"O Syrinx, see and understand the Earth, the marvel of this morning and the circulation of life. Oh, you there and me here! Oh, you! Oh, me! Everything is in Everything!"

"Everything is in Everything! Truly? Oh, these people with formulae! Well, first sing to me of my beauty."

"Oh, yes! This is it!"

She waits up above, standing still, seemingly infinitely comfortable. Pan climbs a nearby tree and, facing her but not within arm's reach, he sits down between two branches, his legs dangling.

He begins, looking her in the eyes for all inspiration: "Very immaculate conception . . . No, no, you see, I can't find anything else."

"I'm waiting; it's only a game, get on with it! When will you tell me about my beauty, if not now? Ah! Describe me, describe me! Be good for something, be my mirror, as human consciousness tries to be that of the indefinite Ideal . . ."

"Oh, not that, my ideal child. It would give you too much right to the ungraspable!" Pedantry—pedantry and a half!

"It's recognized in passing that happiness is the pursuit of the Ideal, and no more."

"To that I can only respond with an impoliteness."

"Speak."

"It's that you're displacing the question, the goal. You're not the goal of my pursuit; in the guise of that very goal, you're only a stage between us. Besides which, it comes to the same thing, since, as long as I don't know you, you are for me the very goal, the Ideal. When I've traversed you, O stage, however absolute, I'll go beyond." Pedantry and a half, the truth entire!

"That's clear, I could easily constrain you to pine away before the illusion of my domain or to jump it. But no, I don't want to be, like you, merely a victim of mutual illusion. At least tell me, first, the color of my illusion."

"Well . . . very immaculate conception . . . I'm closing my eyes: your two large eyes were already there in immortally attentive souls. Diana's sacred bow is not a more definitive inflection than the bow of your mouth. Oh, don't release it! Your large eyes announce something that I shall call Christianity, and you bear your head high like someone who looks above the flocks of Pan to see whether the Messiah isn't coming yet . . ."

Syrinx has sat down on the bank, her legs dangling in the brambles, her perfect and gentle legs with feet shod in white sandals. She is leaning on her right elbow, her head in her hand, offering her large nostalgic and unexplored eyes.

Pan continues to stammer his poverties.

"Everything is in everything! And little Syrinx is a product of the Earth. But no! Is it because, loving you, I can describe your beauty? Wait for me; I'll come to join you . . . no, no, stay! You're beautiful, you're spontaneously perfect! Your organs respire the price of natural immortality. We'll gallop in perpetual betrothal in the brambles of the mountains. Oh, how beautiful you must be in the hunt!"

"The hunt! To the hunt!" clamors Syrinx, who, divinized by that appeal, has leapt to her feet and resumes her gallop toward the day, uttering the clamors of a Valkyrie.

> *Hoyotoho!*
> *Heiaha!*
> *Hahet! Heiaho! Hoyohei!*

It is beginning again. Before descending from his pitiful tree, Pan has to observe the direction that her beauty has taken. Then he has to return toward her, to scale the bank at the side by the gentle slope. But indignation animates him with a primitive ardor. Caliban awakes! He utters the harsh bark of a poor misunderstood bear that has been made to dance too many tricks. The child, in her divine bounds, has a long start, but it's only a matter of time.

And the legendary pursuit of the nymph Syrinx by the god Pan continues, in the overwhelming afternoon, which will end up by melting into evening . . .

She is Woman, that is certain now. He will have her, he will have her! It will be out there, on the summit of that blue-tinted hill, at the most; or rather, at the bottom of the valley thereafter, and he will make her afraid in the depths of a lair he knows, where one slips in the humidity. Everything is in everything, and he will force her to cry *Aditi!* After all, it's him who will end up begging pardon, but no matter. Oh, Diana, with her pale discobolus, can rise this evening, she will see beauties! It isn't for nothing that everything is in Everything.

They traverse the great pine-woods in claustral kilometric solitudes where it has been dark since the beginning of the world when God said "Let there be light!" And the divine bounding child fills those grandiose corridors with intractable clamors:

> *Hoyotoho!*
> *Heiaha!*
> *Hahet! Heiaho! Hoyohei!*

"O appeals of glory and happiness! How she has understood me! To the hunt! To the hunt! Oh, now I understand you, you only want to be happy at bay with your feet bloody! Oh, go on, I shall staunch the blood of your heroic feet and wash your pure and perfect limbs and rock you all night long singing *Aditi!* At the top of the blue-tinted hill we shall light the evening fires. And it will be for ever and ever! And all Olympus will talk about the genius of Pan and his amours, so new, so full of a modern character. Oh, how precious she will be in the coming autumn, in the fall of the leaves that no one has yet understood! Oh, it's necessary that I perfect my pipe for that season and that it finally sings at the first snows the thing that is the thing. *Hoyotoho!* Flee, flee, keep going! Evening isn't falling yet."

And in order to let his fiancée breathe a little, Pan, having arrived at the top of a hill overlooking a new plain, calls a halt. The fiancée turns around momentarily, astonished. Has he had enough? Does he want to renounce the game? She has no confidence; she sets off again. *Hoyotoho!* Evening isn't falling yet.

At one point in the plain there is the dazzling marble square of a tomb. Syrinx stops there for a minute, leaning over as if to smell a flower, then utters a sniggering *Heiaha!* and resumes her beautiful flight in divine bounds.

Heiaha, then! Pan comes down the hill and resumes the equally divine bounds of his pursuit.

He stops momentarily in his turn at the white marble tomb. Like the object of his pursuit he leans over; there is no flower to smell, but this inscription to meditate: *Et in Arcadia Ego*. I too have lived in Arcadia.

Poor mortals, how many reasons they have to love one another!

But Pan and Syrinx are immortal; there is no urgency.

The plan extends all the way to the blue-tinted hill, as vast as an afternoon that will finish by melting into the evening. The *Hoyotohos* and the *Heiahas* become rarer. There is a plain!

What a plain . . . !

What a plain . . . !

And gradually, for everything progresses, the sun declines. The poor nymph senses the dusk coming that is weaving the invisible mesh of its nets. Syrinx loses ground; and the blue-tinted hill to climb will soon be here, doubtless palisaded by atrocious brambles.

Oh, in the brambles, the brambles she will crawl as much as she can, and she will be all bloody, and he will take pity on her

"She's weakening, she's weakening! She doesn't want to abandon herself! She takes me for a lustful Caliban. Oh, kneeling, I shall staunch the blood of your feet. Oh, I shall touch her hair, and pass a finger several times over her delicate arm, and make her occupy herself with me. I shall be able to take her by tenderness and a few fatalistic considerations. It will also be necessary to occupy myself with dinner. Oh, I'll confound her with many little contradictory attentions. It's necessary that she weep and sob infinite pleas for forgiveness.

"Here comes the shepherd's hour!"

The sun makes adieux, or rather says *au revoir*, without hypertrophic mannerisms—the weather is fine! The landscapes begin to quiver and languish in belated tenderness.

The poplar trembles, a tree so distinguished that it chooses its hour. And the weeping willow weeps over the unreasoned burnishing of the mirror of its waters. The hills and the distances darken with anxious solitude. The frogs are about to commence singing, and the stars will not be long delayed; the stars cannot be long delayed. Only the Angelus is lacking—other times, other mores—but, O twilight! Innocence at fraternity by the grace of God! O altars, does not the Unknown remain with it, and peace on earth to couples of good will.

O sheaves of one passed, so-called native land, false convalescences! Soon, it will be night, and the glow-worm will do his work, and the owl will have his say.

But, thank God, one can still see clearly, and the young woman keeps on, and swears to scale the imminent hill, however little that delays the cleaving of her life in two.

She knows the twilight that strangles the *Heiahas* in the throat. She knows that when the net of night has been thrown, it then requires nothing less than the moonlight of Artemis Vigilant to cleanse by her inundation all of that field-hospital. She goes on, she goes on!

She arrives at the hill . . .

O twilight, you don't touch me, you will never touch me! Positive sensuality cannot filter into the ciborium of my being! But who is that whispering there?

Ah, and alas! Three times alas! The individual who is whispering there is a treacherous river, behind those reeds, vague and profound, which forbids access to the foot of the hill. Its vague water, in the twilight . . .

Syrinx parts the reeds and sees the river, the broad and mortuary silence. And Pan arrives! The man is there, drunk on the night!

He is there; Syrinx turns round and raises her hand toward him. He stops at a distance.

How beautiful she is in the evening thus! What to believe?

"Will you please forget me?"

"Oh, forgive me, forgive me! You can see that I'm not in this for nothing. But forget you? I love you, you're my goal, I'm me, and dusk is falling. Let me take charge of explaining everything to you. Oh, what is it that disgusts you about me? Oh, heath for hearth! What, don't you respire this summer night through all your free organs? O summer night, unknown malady, how you do us harm! Myself, I no longer sense anything but us! O rich summer night, I recall now the intoxicating stories Bacchus told me about his conquest of India. I remember, and cannot tear myself away from Delphi! Oh, fury of the shrill flute cleaving the sulfurous storm of the end of the day of the vintage and summoning the lustral downpours! Thyrses and tangled hair! Mysteries of Ceres, mysteries and celebrations, and the common grave! Astarté! Astaroth! Derceto! Adonaï! The round dances in the meadow, already warm, with all the tents of the Shulamites, to the charivari of all the Salammboesque flutes! Everything is in everything!"

"Don't come any closer! What I respire is the jealous and nostalgic admiration of fortunate beings and things, for the one who passes, who passes alone and intact, toward the moonlight of mountains, whose amours are not tomorrows, but only late nights."

"Certainly you are perfect thus and that armor fits you like a glove. But what about the autumn that is coming, poor darling? Will your heart not respire the mortality of the landscapes until the coughing reaches its depths?"

"I shall huddle in a burrow that we have in Hyrcania and only come out *Hoyotoho!* in order to sate myself *Hoyohei!* through the serene manna of snowfall!"

"Yes, doubtless, autumn is still far away; will it ever return? But how full the present night of summer is! O

Syrinx, I cannot go away like that! I cannot forget you after today, O consoler of all my excessive genius! Oh, everything is in Everything, however! And you will not make me believe that you are above it. See, already, these flashes of heat! Astarté, Adonaï. God wills it!"

"*Hoyotoho!* Don't come any closer! *Heiaha! Heiaha!* Help! Child, how can you not see that sensuality is desire, that happiness is passing and causing desire in couples overwhelmed by happiness?

"Well, so be it, I shall die; I who would have cared for you so well! My madness is divine, certainly, but not as much as the price of your will. Forgive me, forgive me, I shall die sweetly. I shall render my soul into my elementary and primitive two-sou pipe, singing the exile with which your vision honors me."

"You can see clearly yourself; there is nothing but art; art is desire perpetuated . . ."

Oh, for once, she has said that in a tone so equivocally charitable that Pan no longer hesitates, is no longer able to hesitate! Head lowered, arms open, he advances resolutely upon her. Her, a weak woman, now only worthy of that name, tracked and caught thus in the indifference of beautiful twilight!

With a supreme burst of inhumanity, of all the immortal virginity of her eyes facing him, Syrinx holds Pan back again for a second, clamors a last *Hoyotoho!* And then throws herself into the thin curtain of reeds and lets herself fall in the water.

And the amorous genius, who has bounded, is only clasping in his sincere arms the plume of dry roses. He parts them, and looks, and sees the beautiful saved child who has been received, so white in their white arms, by silent naiads, who draw her away in silent lines.

Those momentary frolics have scarcely rippled the crepuscular surface of the slow and mortuary river under the beautiful evening sky.

It is done without a word. It is finished.

And it is evening, the evening that does not bring counsel.

Oh, out there, facing him, at the level of the water, is that still her adored head that is gazing, still motionless, or simply a bouquet of water-lilies playing in its fashion?

It's over; the river is asleep.

She was a true virgin and surely a sign of new times.

Then Pan, without deciding to quit with his eyes the tomb of his contradictory dream, at that revelation of new times for which his genius will perhaps be insufficient, emits a sigh, a melancholy "oh!" so adorably young, an "oh" so disinterested after that long day, an "oh" so inviolably inconsolable and misunderstood, so innocently unique! Oh, it was, so very fortunately, one of those "ohs" that are no longer heard, in spite of all that the new times bring, and now a musical voice rises, exhaled by that bouquet of water-lilies opposite and slides over the mortuary river and says: "O breezes, come on, hang on, give me back my soul."

And a certain breeze glides, which comes to execute things in smooth rustles in the curtain of reeds with tall hollow stems, with long silky leaves and singing plumes.

Things, that breeze of soul in the reeds! Pan pricks up his pointed ears.

O smooth rustles, winged kisses, flourishes of rumor, fans pulverizing in chorus a fountain in the depths of the gardens of Armida, the crumpled handkerchiefs of fays, the silence that dreams aloud, a sponge passed over all poetry!

And it whispers, mercifully: "Quickly, quickly, friend, it's her soul that is passing in those reeds that you hold!"

With both hands, Pan compresses his heart, more divine than ever; he wipes away a tear, throws his old pipe into the tomb of the river and, by virtue of a universal inspiration, without hesitation, without scratching his ear or tugging his pointed beard, he gives the accolade to those enchanted reeds, and then cuts three stems, from which he makes seven pipes of decreasing length, which he hollows out, empties of their pith, pierces with holes and binds together with two rushes.

And it is well and truly a flute of a new kind!

Pan runs his desiccated lips over it in the hope of kisses, and what he draws from the flute is a miraculous scale of the new era, declaring naively the happiness of the flute, its happiness in coming into the world on that beautiful evening of the Pastoral Age.

Pan, laughing through his tears, turns the new flute over and over in his thick Caliban fingers, the flute with seven pipes, the divine Syrinx.

"Oh! Thank you, thank you! Seven pipes!"

But it is already pitch dark, and the bouquet of water-lilies has faded away.

Pan sits down in the reeds, plays a prelude repeatedly, and presses the toy to his heart, and brushes it with his thick lips. Then he meditates.

Night has fallen. Nothing can be seen any longer but the solitude of the country; nothing can be heard any longer but the freshness of the river. O memorable attentive night, let's go!

Pan commences: "O my hymn, develop yourself on yourself and not in advance, as terrestrial consciousness has to do, if it doesn't want to break the spell and close the beautiful eyes of Maia the Comfortable forever."

And at first there are funambulistic trills, stabbing, spasmodic, profligate, which yap and then die away, expiring in a pious rosary of recovery.

Then an isolated and tenuous note rises, as calm as an aerostat above a crowd of idlers.

And that is the song, in kilometers, as pale as a churching ballad, suddenly interrupted by a heavy scale, like a bell knocking over excessively hasty scaffolding, then unwrapped and developing in a garland around a pedestal awaiting its statue, which will fortunately never, ever come.

And then, pell-mell: introits rising up in a deluge, kyries in waterless caravans, offertories in malnutrition, orisons chilled and fallen very low, excessively facile litanies, magnificats going into detail, foaming misereres and stabats around a crib, around a cistern in which the Lunar Diana is reflected.

Pan wipes his lips with the back of his hand, puts down his flute for a moment, and speaks.

214

"I'm all alone; my song is monotonous, for I only know how to love and, my fiancée having gone away, I can only groan until further orders. Oh, what a day has passed! O Syrinx, have I dreamed you? I recall her minute by minute and word by word, and her fashion of gazing, and the angle of inclination of her neck and the sound of her voice, and yet I haven't seen her and I haven't heard her. And that's once again that I haven't had the presence of mind to penetrate the face of the presence of things. I could have looked at her and listened to her forever and taken her formula from life. Instead of that, I thought—about what? About everything. And it passed. Oh, am I then incurably in Everything? How insouciant I am! Oh, who will throw a bridge between my heart and the present? If she had only left me a lock of her hair that I could hold on my lips as evidence."

He took up his flute with seven pipes, his talismanic flute, the soul of Syrinx, and put it to his lips. And as on such a beautiful evening of the Pastoral Age it is permissible to repeat oneself, it is the Stabat again, the Stabat around a cistern in which Lunar Diana is reflected.

He raises his eyes; the Moon, there she is! Glorious and palpable, roundly blinding, rising from the melancholy and pure horizon above a black line of hills.

Pan hurries his Stabat and starts to fulminate an imprecation against Diana:

"*Hoyotoho* up there, O Moon, aegis of ice, color of camphor!

"O Diana, your divinity leaves me cold; I have seen nothing in your vices of conformation.

"And why have you dressed yourself with a sex? What shame to conserve futile organs of impurity! Or rather, what a scantly immortal chastity that has need, in order to hold firm, to attract by those lures the repugnant and satisfying spectacle of the male rendered beside himself, the male enslaved!

"And where do you get that immortality? From a great amour, interred or impossible? But no! You have not dreamed of our sex, our so legitimate sex! No, you were brought up in the forests, and great hunts in every season, and the rude bristles of wild boar, and blood and barking dogs, and the cold water of springs in the depths of the woods. You are a man, a sublime and pale man, a planter with poor white slaves, and you whip your hunting companions cruelly, and by means of inadmissible incantations you cauterize their poor sex organs in the depths of the claustral forest. Oh, get away, I know everything! I'm not hallucinated. Everything is in Everything, and I am the brave empirical sentinel!"

But the Moon remains there, roundly blinding, alone in all the sky . . .

And Pan, who is shivering with fever, falls into dreams, into Thousand-and-One-Nights abjection, in the evening breeze that wanders, wanders carrying the breath of every corner, the bleating of every bosom, the sighs of every weather-vane, the aromas of every bandage, the rustle of all the scarves lost in the brambles of the high roads.

O lunar enchantment! Ecstatic climate! Is this really sure? Is this the Annunciation? Is it not merely the story of a summer evening?

And Pan, bounding like a madman, without having said adieu to the dead river, pressing his new flute against his wounded side, departs again at a gallop in the lunar enchantment toward his valley, piloted by the Moon, luckily!

Fortunately, and henceforth, it will be sufficient for him, in bad hours, to draw a nostalgic scale from his Syrinx, in order to redirect his large and united eyes, with his head held high, toward the Ideal, the master of us all.

ACKNOWLEDGEMENTS

PAUL ADAM (1862-1920) was imprisoned when his first novel, *Chair molle* (1885) was prosecuted for obscenity, but went on to a successful and prolific career. After his early association with Jean Moréas and Gustave Kahn, he devoted himself primarily to writing novels, deliberately attempting to fuse and hybridize Symbolist and Naturalist techniques; he is now best known for historical novels set during the Napoleonic Wars. His novels often include interludes of utopian speculation, and he wrote one of the most important utopian texts of the *fin de siècle* in *Lettres de Malaisie* (1898; tr. as "Letters from Malaisie"), which makes extravagant use of graphic symbolism. "Vénus et le faun" first appeared in *Le Journal* 27 June 1902. "Venus and the Faun" appears here for the first time.

FRÉDÉRIC BOUTET (1874-1941) hung out at Le Chat Noir and befriended Oscar Wilde in his youth. His first collection of stories, *Contes de la nuit* (1898; second ed. 1903) was set very solidly in the Decadent and Symbolist tradition, and the novellas *L'Homme Savage et Julius Pingouin* (1902; tr. as the title stories of *The Antisocial Man and Other Strange Stories* and *The Voyage of Julius Pingouin and Other Strange Stories*, 2013) are also striking exercises in Symbolist fiction, but the pressure of making a living forced his work to become more commercial and the baroque aspects of his style and subject matter gradually faded away. "Gabrielle et son faun" first appeared in *Le Français* in 1903 before being reprinted in *Histoires vraisemblables* (1903). "Gabrielle and her Faun" was first published in *The Voyage of Julius Pingouin and Other Strange Stories*.

LÉON CLADEL (1834-1892) was a friend of Charles Baudelaire, who provided a preface for his first novel, *Les Martyrs ridicules* (1862). Like another friend, Catulle Mendès, and Paul Adam he was imprisoned for offending public morals in *Une Maudite* (1876). The original version of "Aegipan" was published in the collection *Quelques sires* (1885), where the date of its composition is given as 1860; the translation appears here for the first time.

GASTON DERYS (1875-1945) began writing under the aegis of the Symbolist movement but became a prolific writer of ephemeral popular fiction, non-fiction and dramatic works. "L'Outrage punie" was originally published in *La Lanterne* 9 January 1904; "The Punished Outrage" appears here for the first time.

ANATOLE FRANCE (1844-1924) inherited the mantle of the greatest living French writer after the death of Victor Hugo, and won the Nobel Prize for Literature in 1921. *Thaïs* (1890), a classical fantasy in the tradition of Gustave Flaubert's *La Tentation de*

Saint-Antoine (1874), was followed by the collection *L'Étui de nacre* (1892; tr. as *Mother of Pearl*), which includes a further exercise in the same vein, "Amycus et Célestin," and laid the foundations for the more flamboyant collection *Le Puits de Sainte Clare* (1895; tr. as *The Well of Saint Clare*), which contains "Saint-Satyre." The version of "Amycus and Célestin" included here is original; the version of "Saint Satyr" is revised from an earlier translation featured in *The Second Dedalus Book of Decadence: The Black Feast* (1992).

REMY DE GOURMONT (1858-1915) was the most important literary critic of his era, and his studies of authors involved in the Symbolist Movement, many of them collected in *Le Livre des masques* (1896) and *Le Deuxième Livre des Masques* (1898), provided an invaluable map of its extent and commentary on its ambitions. He was one of the founders of the *Mercure de France* and became its most prolific contributor, developing his distinctively mannered short fiction in its pages. Disfigured by lupus, he became a recluse before the century ended, and his health deteriorated steadily thereafter, although he kept on writing relentlessly while he could. "Le Faune" appeared in *Histoires magiques* (1894). "The Faun" is extensively revised from the version that appeared in *The Angels of Perversity* (1992).

JULES LAFORGUE (1860-1887), born in Uruguay of French parents, was taken under the wing of Paul Bourget, editor of *La Vie moderne*, in 1880 and began to frequent Le Chat Noir with the Hydropathes, but got a job working for the Empress Augusta and lived in Berlin from 1881 to 1886. When he returned to Paris he threw himself into the burgeoning Symbolist Movement wholeheartedly, but he died of tuberculosis a year later. He left for posthumous publication a classic collection of satirical stories, *Moralités legendaries* (1887), in which "Pan et la syrinx" was reprinted, having first appeared in *La Revue Indépendante* in July 1887; the translation is original to the present volume.

MAURICE LEBLANC (1864-1941) was a prolific writer of short fiction and novels, who attained little success until he began chronicling the adventures of the professional criminal and amateur detective Arsène Lupin in 1905, in reaction against the colossal popularity of Sherlock Holmes, which eventually filled more than twenty volumes. "Les Portes de Saint-Maclou" first appeared in *Gil Blas* 30 May 1900. "The Doors of Saint-Maclou" is original to the present volume.

MAURICE MAGRE (1877-1941) was a prolific poet, novelist and dramatist with strong Decadent affiliations, perhaps the finest French writer of fantastic fiction in the first half of the twentieth century. A twelve-volume set of translations of his work appeared from Black Coat Press in 2017-18 but does not include "Le Dernier faun" which was first published in the *Le Petit Parisen, supplément littéraire illustré*, 11 June 1905. "The Last Faun" is original to the present volume.

CATULLE MENDÈS (1841-1909) came to Paris in 1859, and was taken under the wing of Théophile Gautier. His unproduced drama *Roman d'une nuit* (1861) was prosecuted for obscenity, landing him in prison for a month. He was extraordinarily adaptable and prolific, producing an enormous amount of short fiction for newspapers. His novels *Zo'har* (1886) and *Méphistophela* (1890; tr. as *Mephistophela*) were crucial contributions to the Decadent Movement. "Le Petit Faune" first appeared in *La Revue populaire* novembre 1882 under the pseudonym Jean-Qui-Passe, and was reprinted in *Pour lire au bain* (1888; tr. as *To Read in the Bath*); "Sous les laurier roses" also appeared in that volume. "The Little Faun" appeared in *Symbolism and Decadence: A Showcase Anthology* (Snuggly, 2018) before appearing in the translation of the collection, in which "Under the Oleanders" appeared for the first time.

MAURICE MONTEGUT (1855-1911) was a prolific writer of prose and dramas, associated in the early part of his career with the Parnassian Movement along with Catulle Mendès. His first collection of poetry was *La Bohème sentimentale* (1875). "L'Île des satyres" appeared in *Gil Blas* 17 July 1891; "The Isle of Satyrs" is original to the present volume.

HENRI DE RÉGNIER (1864-1936) formed a friendship at school with Egbert Viélé, who began signing himself Francis Viélé-Griffin when the two of them became Symbolist poets; the two founded *Entretiens politiques et littéraires* in collaboration with Paul Adam in 1890.

Regnier published his own "Symbolist Manifesto" in *Le Bosquet de Psyché* (1894) and several collections of Symbolist prose, most notably *La Canne de jaspe* (1897), which included "La Mort de Monsieur de Nouâtre et de Madame de Ferlinde." "Hésitation sentimentale" was first published in *La Presse* 9 January 1923. "The Death of Monsieur de Nouatre and Madame de Ferlinde" first appeared in *A Surfeit of Mirrors: Symbolist Tales and Uncertain Stories* (2012); "Sentimental Hesitation" is original to the present volume.

J. H. ROSNY was the pseudonym of the Belgian-born Joseph-Henri Boex (1856-1940), shared for a while with his brother Justin; after the split he began signing himself J. H. Rosny aîné [the elder]. He was best known as a Naturalist writer, but was also an important contributor to the French genre of *roman scientifique*, and he published three lush antiquarian fantasies, including *Le Flûte de Pan* (1897), under the pseudonym Enacryos. "Pan's Flute" first appeared in *Pan's Flute and Other Stories* (2018).

SAINT-BLANCARD was the signature attached to "Le Masque du faune" in *Gil Blas* 30 May 1900. The aristocratic signature was employed at that time by Jehan de Gontaut-Biron, Marquis de Saint-Blancard (1865-1937), who also signed himself Marquis de Gontaut Saint-Blancard, but it might also have been employed by other members of the family, including his wife, Elisabeth Ferron de La Ferronaye (1870-1951). "The Mask of the Faun" is original to the present volume.

ALBERT SAMAIN (1858-1900) was a Symbolist poet heavily influenced by Baudelaire and Verlaine, who used to recite his work in Le Chat Noir, and cultivated a reputation for morbid nostalgia. "Hyalis le petit faune aux yeux bleus" was first published posthumously in *Contes* (1902) and frequently reprinted in isolation thereafter as an illustrated children's book. "Hyalis the Blue-Eyed Faun" is original to the present volume.

THÉO VARLET (1878-1938) was a prolific poet and translator who found it convenient to reside in the Midi, where the climate allowed him to pursue his interest in nudism more comfortably. As a prose writer he made important contributions to the genre of *roman scientifique*. He was also a committed pacifist and an enthusiastic experimenter with opium and other psychotropic substances. "Le Dernier Satyre" was the title story of his first collection of short stories, published in 1905. "The Last Satyr" was first published in *The Golden Rock* (2012).

A PARTIAL LIST OF SNUGGLY BOOKS

G. ALBERT AURIER *Elsewhere and Other Stories*

S. HENRY BERTHOUD *Misanthropic Tales*

LÉON BLOY *The Desperate Man*

LÉON BLOY *The Tarantulas' Parlor and Other Unkind Tales*

ÉLÉMIR BOURGES *The Twilight of the Gods*

JAMES CHAMPAGNE *Harlem Smoke*

FÉLICIEN CHAMPSAUR *The Latin Orgy*

FÉLICIEN CHAMPSAUR
    The Emerald Princess and Other Decadent Fantasies

BRENDAN CONNELL *Clark*

BRENDAN CONNELL *Unofficial History of Pi Wei*

RAFAELA CONTRERAS *The Turquoise Ring and Other Stories*

ADOLFO COUVE *When I Think of My Missing Head*

QUENTIN S. CRISP *Aiaigasa*

QUENTIN S. CRISP *Graves*

LADY DILKE *The Outcast Spirit and Other Stories*

CATHERINE DOUSTEYSSIER-KHOZE *The Beauty of the Death Cap*

ÉDOUARD DUJARDIN *Hauntings*

BERIT ELLINGSEN *Now We Can See the Moon*

BERIT ELLINGSEN *Vessel and Solsvart*

ENRIQUE GÓMEZ CARRILLO *Sentimental Stories*

EDMOND AND JULES DE GONCOURT *Manette Salomon*

REMY DE GOURMONT *From a Faraway Land*

GUIDO GOZZANO *Alcina and Other Stories*

EDWARD HERON-ALLEN *The Complete Shorter Fiction*

RHYS HUGHES *Cloud Farming in Wales*

J.-K. HUYSMANS *Knapsacks*

COLIN INSOLE *Valerie and Other Stories*

JUSTIN ISIS *Pleasant Tales II*

JUSTIN ISIS (editor) *Marked to Die: A Tribute to Mark Samuels*

JUSTIN ISIS AND DANIEL CORRICK (editors)
    Drowning in Beauty: The Neo-Decadent Anthology

www.ingramcontent.com/pod-product-compliance
Lightning Source LLC
Chambersburg PA
CBHW022024120726
47898CB00007BA/2455